The thin sliver of space between them heated with their breaths.

Trystan lifted one hand, sketching the backs of his knuckles along her cheekbone. Her pulse quickened, her body tingling, and she tipped her head into his caress.

Isabeau swallowed, holding his gaze. Felt the air become heavy with awareness until—yes—her lips found his. That spark exploded as she tasted him. His hands felt like magic gliding down her back, the silk of her dress caressing her skin along with each stroke of his fingers.

With a whispery moan, she angled closer to him, the warm wall of his body a perfect fit against her. He deepened the kiss, his hold both strong and careful, the taste of him delicious. Her thoughts scrambled as Trystan's touch drove her need higher, made her want more.

Want everything.

* * *

The Love Child is part of the Alaskan Oil Barons series, the eight-book saga from *USA TODAY* bestselling au...

Dear Reader,

Welcome to the third book in my Alaskan Oil Barons family saga!

This book features a subject very dear to my heart—service dogs. I'm an active volunteer with Palmetto Animal Assisted Life Services (PAALS), an ADI-accredited service dog training organization in Columbia, South Carolina. In looking for more ways to help, I donated the naming rights to a dog in one of my books as a PAALS fund-raiser. The couple that generously won the auction chose the name Paige, after their beloved rat terrier. The Paige in this book is a Labrador retriever and performs a different service than PAALS dogs, but the beautiful bond between a handler and service dog is universal. It's an honor to showcase that connection in this story.

Thank you for diving into the adventures in my Alaskan Oil Barons series. I hope you enjoy Trystan, Isabeau and Paige's journey!

Cheers,

Catherine Mann

PS: PAALS is a 501(c)(3) nonprofit organization and ADI accredited. For more information about the PAALS mission, visit www.paals.org.

CATHERINE MANN

THE LOVE CHILD

Recycling programs
for this product may
not exist in your area.

ISBN-13: 978-1-335-97144-9

The Love Child

Printed in U.S.A.

USA TODAY bestselling author **Catherine Mann** has won numerous awards for her novels, including both a prestigious RITA® Award and an *RT Book Reviews* Reviewers' Choice Award. After years of moving around the country bringing up four children, Catherine has settled in her home state of South Carolina, where she's active in animal rescue. For more information, visit her website, catherinemann.com.

Books by Catherine Mann

Harlequin Desire

Diamonds in the Rough

One Good Cowboy
Pursued by the Rich Rancher
Pregnant by the Cowboy CEO

The Lourdes Brothers of Key Largo

The Boss's Baby Arrangement
His Secretary's Little Secret

Alaskan Oil Barons

The Baby Claim
The Double Deal
The Love Child

Visit her Author Profile page at Harlequin.com, or catherinemann.com, for more titles.

To the Palmetto Animal Assisted
Life Services (PAALS) and Jennifer Rogers
(executive director and founder)

One

"Spread your legs wider, please, Mr. Mikkelson."

Isabeau Waters rocked back on her heels, staring up the length of the Mikkelson oil magnate looming over her.

She'd spent countless hours in the company of naked and near-naked men in her profession as a media image consultant. But never in her job had she revamped the wardrobe for a man who tempted her quite so much, for so long, as Alaskan mogul and rancher Trystan Mikkelson.

Measuring his inseam? Heaven help her.

Kneeling on the plush carpet in the luxurious office space, Isabeau adjusted her grip on the measuring tape. She worked her way up his long, denim-clad legs until her eyes were level with his...leather belt. So close she could read the inscription on the Iditarod sled dog racing belt buckle.

Exhale.

Think.

Be a professional.

This job was high-paying and high-profile. The merger of the powerful Mikkelson and Steele family businesses into Alaska Oil Barons, Incorporated, had dominated stock exchange news, causing the market to fluctuate. Shares had only just begun to steady when the Steele patriarch suffered a major injury in a horseback-riding accident.

Now the two factions were working overtime to make sure the company presented a cohesive image when it came to leadership. With so many offspring on both sides, Isabeau was still stunned that this man, who preferred running the family's ranch up in Alaska's north country, was their pick to be the face of the merged company. Apparently, siblings on both sides of the family were having marriage troubles, health issues or were too shy to speak in public, leaving them with only this rugged Mikkelson cowboy and a teenage Steele kid to choose from. Since the teenager was obviously not an option, that left Trystan Mikkelson.

For now, anyway.

Her mission? To make him over. His wardrobe was

easy enough. The tougher part though? To keep him in-line and on-message for the next four weeks until the Wilderness Preservation Initiative Fund-raiser— a wine and dine with celebrities. Then stay on until his mother's wedding to the Steele oil magnate, Jack.

She'd done this pre-assessment routine time and time again, with many different kinds of people. But as she took note of his measurements, her eyes falling to his angular jaw… Well keeping *herself* on-message seemed like it would be the true work.

He shifted from one dusty boot to the other. "No disrespect to your profession, ma'am, but I'm not going to be trussed up like some pretty boy."

"I will keep your wardrobe preferences in mind as I order pieces and talk to the tailor. You will still be you, but a version of you that inspires confidence from less…rugged investors." Isabeau tucked a stray hair behind her ear, fingers barely grazing the pearl drop earrings her best friend had given her when she'd launched her image consulting company. A gesture of good luck, and Isabeau had made it a ritual to always wear them to the first fitting.

He grunted.

She rolled her eyes. "Use your words, please."

"Excuse me?" He raised one dark brow. "I'm not a damn toddler."

She agreed one hundred percent with that.

"Exactly. The stakes are much higher than a time-out. Alaska Oil Barons, Inc., has hired me to do a job." And that job apparently was going to include polishing his words as well as his wardrobe.

Although she could tell he'd made an attempt at spiffing up today. But based on comparison to photos she'd researched of him online, *spiffing* for him meant swapping worn, faded flannel with a fresh-out-of-the-package plaid. She appreciated the effort. Not that she'd suffered any illusions that this would be an easy gig.

For more reasons than one.

Keeping her professional distance around this hulking sexy distraction would be a challenge, to say the least.

Eyes upward. A much safer option.

Maybe.

He was grinning, damn him.

His thick hair looked perpetually rumpled by the wind into a dusty brown storm. A part of her grieved over his impending appointment with the barber. But she needed that hair to be a bit more tamed. The man too.

His broad shoulders and chest were sculpted with muscles born of hard work rather than in a gym. She would need to order larger suit jackets and his tuxedo would need to be custom-made.

He was all man, and her mouth watered with desire.

Totally unprofessional and barely controllable.

She reined her thoughts in, focusing on getting her notes in place. Nabbing Alaska Oil Barons, Inc., was a coup. They were a big-time client for her, and the merger of the Mikkelson and Steele companies made the corporation all the more newsworthy right now. The business still operated out of two office buildings where the Steeles and Mikkelsons once had their individual spaces. Today, she was in the Mikkelson space.

Jeannie Mikkelson's office to be exact—Trystan's office for now, since his mother was plastered to her new fiancé's side while Jack Steele recovered from surgery after a horseback-riding accident. The spacious office was gorgeous and one Isabeau would give her eyeteeth to have, but she had to confess it didn't fit Trystan Mikkelson. From the cream-colored office chair to the sea foam–colored furniture with teal accents, it was more of a woman's space.

Trystan's eyes kept shifting to the windows along the wall and the skylight, as if he was considering an escape route to the great outdoors he was reputed to prefer.

She glanced down to jot additional notes for short-term and long-term goals. First order of business, getting Trystan properly outfitted for his sister Glenna's wedding to the oldest Steele brother, Broderick, this weekend.

As CFOs, Glenna and Broderick were the obvious ones to take the helm of the company for now, but they were emphatic that their relationship deserved to come first. The other Mikkelson

son, Charles, Jr., insisted the same for his troubled marriage. And while Isabeau applauded their devotion to their spouses, and she intended to spin their choices well in the press releases, she also wanted to shake every one of them for not recognizing how tenuous things were with the merger right now.

Stockholders needed reassurance. Panic was a dangerous emotion.

Her thoughts somersaulted away from the task at hand, her mind's eye turning to Paige, her Labrador retriever, who'd stretched beneath the sofa, only her head and paws sticking out. As if the dog could sense Isabeau's attention, Paige raised her head, those wide brown eyes sympathetic and reassuring all at once. Paige cocked her head, ears flopping and fur rustling against the red vest that proclaimed her a service dog in huge black capital letters. In a smaller, less sprawling font, was the instructive Do Not Pet. Isabeau needed Paige to alert her to diabetic issues.

And anxiety attacks.

But Isabeau preferred to keep her reasons for having a service dog as private as possible. Panic attacks played a major role in why she chose to be a behind-the-scenes media person rather than working in front of the cameras. Her stalker boyfriend from college was in prison now, but the fear remained close.

Clearing her throat, she held up the tape measure again, standing. "Almost finished."

"Glad to know." He stretched his arms wide as she measured across his chest.

She considered herself a professional. She'd never had a problem with desiring a client before, while on the job.

It was going to be a long month completing her contract.

But this gig would cement her reputation, and it carried the potential to land her more clients of this caliber. She had only herself to depend on—no family, no fat inheritance. Her health was stable for now, but her diabetes had sidelined her before. She needed to build a cushion of savings for emergencies.

Never would she be like her mother, flat broke and alone.

"Mr. Mikkelson, you need—"

"Trystan," he insisted in that gravelly voice of his, a melodic rumble.

"Trystan," she conceded. "You need to weigh your words carefully. Less is more, which actually, now that I think about it, should be an easier path for you. Just no impulsive outbursts. It's easier to add to a statement than to walk back a negative impression."

"It's just a fund-raiser. I've been attending them my whole life."

"You're more than attending now. You're the figurehead of the company, a company with a president that almost died when he broke his spine in the middle of a major merger." She reminded him of what he should clearly be keeping top-of-mind but still seemed to disregard. "If you really prefer not to do this, I could talk to your family about one of the Steele siblings taking over the public role—heaven knows there are plenty of them…"

"No, I've got this." He pulled a tight smile. "The fact that there are so damn many of them is just the reason I need to do this. To make sure my mother keeps her equal stake in the company and those Steeles don't edge her out."

"I hear you, and I understand your point. But you do know that is exactly the sort of thing you shouldn't say in public."

"United front. Got it." He tapped his temple. "We're all supposed to ignore the fact that our families have been at war for longer than I can remember. I'm supposed to forget all the times my father called Jack Steele a ruthless crook."

She leveled a glare at him. "Mr. Mikkelson—"

"Trystan." His eyes were robin's-egg blue, a beautiful, vibrant hue in this otherwise stark man. "And yes, I know that's another thing I'm not supposed to say."

Those. Eyes.

This. Man.

Heaven help her.

It was going to be a long month.

* * *

All for family.

That'd been Trystan's motto his whole life. And it was why he stood, albeit begrudgingly, getting a damn makeover.

His clothes shouldn't matter. He had a business degree and ran a multimillion-dollar ranching operation. All of which he'd accomplished in jeans and dusty boots rather than suits and polished wing tips. But his family's livelihood was on the line.

He would do whatever it took to stabilize the newly formed Alaska Oil Barons, Inc.

Even if it meant prancing around like some show horse. Even if he hated every second of the posturing.

Although working with Isabeau Waters certainly made the task bearable.

She was a breath of fresh air. And, yeah, she was very easy on the eyes.

Her red hair shone with hints of gold streaking through. It was gathered on one side so that the rest fell over one shoulder. The natural wave swirled into one big curl that tempted him to tangle his fingers through to test the texture. He was a sensual man, a man of the outdoors who experienced life firsthand rather than sitting behind a desk sifting through the details on a computer screen.

Her eyes were the soft blue of his home state's sky, sparkling and changeable. A deep breath filled him with the scent of her—like the wild irises that bloomed in summer, beautiful and an ironic mix of delicate petals that somehow managed to survive to bloom every year despite the harsh Alaska winters.

He stopped that thought short.

Damn.

Isabeau Waters was making him turn downright poetic.

His gaze turned to the yellow lab staring up at him with inquisitive, chocolate-brown eyes. Though he wanted to fluff the dog's ears, he refrained because the dog was at work. Still, his soul longed for the simplicity of a canine companion here in this unfamiliar situation.

Understanding animals was easy for him. People? Not so much.

He wanted to be on the ranch, riding a horse or even reviewing inventory spreadsheets. The public scene wasn't his forte, not like it was for his older brother Chuck. But Chuck's marriage was on life support, and that relationship was the only thing his older brother valued more than the family business.

Chuck had learned those priorities from their parents, Charles Sr. and Jeannie, a tightly bonded couple until Charles's death. They'd all feared for Jeannie when her husband died of a heart attack over two years ago. They'd prayed she would find a reason to live.

They just hadn't expected her reason would be their family's corporate enemy, Jack Steele.

Trystan had spent his teenage years hearing his father list Jack's many flaws. And now he and his siblings were all expected to just forget that.

The movement of Isabeau's slender body trekking over to the desk, her hair swishing, made him forget all about his family's drama, at least for the moment. She grabbed some binders, flipping to different sections, writing on pages and adding sticky notes. A covert glance over her shoulder, back to him, had his heart pounding.

Why was the most attractive woman he'd met in ages also the person he had to work with? He wanted to flirt with her and take her to dinner instead.

But he would have to give serious thought to the consequences before mixing business and pleasure.

Family always came first.

He'd been adopted by Jeannie and Charles when his own parents had split. His biological parents had married as teens because he was on the way. Their union had been rocky and volatile from the start. After the split, when Trystan was ten, his mother, Jeannie's sister, had been ready to turn him over to foster care. His other aunt had offered to share care of him with Jeannie, but Jeannie had insisted Trystan should have a steady home. She and Charles had welcomed him into their brood.

He knew Jeannie loved him, that she'd accepted him, but he also knew she hadn't had a choice. His other aunt hadn't really been an option as a single mom herself. Taking him in had been the honorable thing for Jeannie and Charles to do.

He owed the Mikkelsons more than he could repay. They'd saved him from an overburdened system where he likely would have ended up in a group home. They'd given him a place in their family. They'd treated him every bit as equally as their three biological children. Now, most people didn't even know or remember he was adopted. Some days he could almost believe he was really one of them rather than a cast-off cousin.

Other times, like now, he was reminded of that debt.

As if she could feel his gaze, Isabeau glanced over her shoulder at him. "If you couldn't be a rancher, what would you do with your life?"

"Why does that matter?" A shrug. No other future mattered, only the present he lived in. That was his life. Walking to the wet bar, Trystan grabbed a beer and twisted the top off. He tipped the bottle's neck to her, inquiring.

A faint smile dusted her lips, but she shook her head, holding up a hand. "No, thank you. And as for the question, I'm just trying to get to know you better, beyond our brief meetings in the past and an internet search on the history of your family. The more I understand you, the more authentic I can be in the choices I make for your image makeover. I truly do want you to be pleased with the decisions.

If it's fake, that will show in your demeanor. People will sense it's a facade."

"Then we're screwed because I'm never going to be a smooth-talking, tuxedo-wearing dude." He took a sip of the beer—his favorite summer ale from his family-owned brewery, Icecap Brews. The crisp, medium-bodied flavor settled him, the aftertaste of wheat drawing out memories of late nights working on the ranch. His sanctuary.

"Trust me. I know what I'm doing." She gestured toward the binders—toward the organized checklists, charts and measures that ought to transform him from rugged recluse to the face of Alaska Oil Barons, Inc.

"Well, then, how would you feel if you couldn't do your job? If someone thrust you into a role you weren't comfortable with?" He took another swig as he leaned against the wall, noticing her confident posture, the way her brows lifted in answer to the challenge he threw at her.

A sassy smile set the corners of her mouth up, reaching those bright blue eyes. "This isn't about me."

"That's a cop-out answer."

"Fine, then. I would search for help. Like how I have my dog here to help me adapt to the curveballs life has thrown my way."

He walked toward where she leaned against the desk, his fingers tracing the corners of the beer bottle's label. Each movement, every step, sparked more static crackling in the air between them. Stopping beside her, he leaned against the desk to her left, aware of the lilac perfume on her skin. "Then what would you do if this profession hadn't worked out for you?"

"I'll answer if you will." Her hand gravitated to his Stetson on the desk, touching the felt lightly. Was she subconsciously drawn to it?

Awareness tumbled through him as he drank in her slender features—the tipped nose, the confidence.

"Fine." He nodded. "You first."

She clicked her tongue. "Testing the trust issue. Okay, I would go back to school and study clothing design. Now your turn."

"Archeology. I can see myself sifting through the earth at an excavation site." He brought the bottle to his lips, imagining what it'd be like to be immersed in an excavation pit in some remote location. No press. Few people. Yeah, he could live like that.

"So you're a patient man with an attention to detail."

His brow raised and he tilted the bottle, which caused the ale to slosh slightly. A contained wave. "I guess you could say that."

"Nice to know. The ideas are churning in my mind already."

She was sure learning a lot about him, and he wasn't finding out a damn thing of importance about her.

He set aside his beer and strode toward the yellow Lab. "Tell me about your dog."

Isabeau's spine went straight and she closed her notebook slowly, her eyes averted. "She's a Labrador retriever, she's three and a half years old, and her name is Paige."

Obvious. But if she didn't want to talk about the fact that Paige wore a service dog vest with patches and lettering, then he wasn't going to be rude. He'd just been trying to make conversation.

Not his strength.

Turning, she flashed an overbright, tense smile. "You can ask. I was just messing with you by giving those obvious answers. Take it as a tip on how to avoid questions you don't want to answer."

"Touché. I apologize if I shouldn't have asked about your working dog. I was just trying to fill the awkward silence. I should have asked about your favorite vacation spot or what made you pick this job or something."

"Those would have been good conversation starters. But I'm comfortable discussing Paige with you. It's more the strangers approaching me with questions that are bothersome. I've even had people accuse her of being a fake working dog since I don't 'appear' disabled." She shook her head, that spiral of red hair sliding along her shoulder. "Paige alerts to my diabetes."

"How did I not know that about you?"

She stacked her binders. "It's not like you and I are besties."

He took another step closer, setting the beer on the desk, the tempting scent of her perfume swirling around him again. "But I know you. Or rather, I've noticed you and for some reason I didn't notice your dog."

"That's a good thing. If she's drawing attention to herself, she's not doing her job. Well, unless I were to be in some kind of health crisis, then she would get help or bring my medication. But she's very good at what she does. Since I've added her to my life, she's kept me from getting so distracted I miss drops or spikes in my glucose level."

"So I shouldn't pet her."

"Not while she's wearing her cape." That tight-lipped, tense smile returned as her head gave a curt, dismissive shake.

"Cape?"

"Vest. She understands that when she's wearing it, she's working. When it's off, she can play like any other dog."

"Ah, okay. Does it bother you that I'm asking about this?" An intrusion into his own life would've been met with some resistance if the roles were reversed. And the last thing he wanted to do was make Isabeau feel isolated.

"Actually, no. It's good to have something to talk about while I work."

"How does she detect your blood sugar?"

"She senses it by smell."

"Like a drug dog?"

"Or hunting dog, or search-and-rescue dog. Same premise, but fine-tuned. Not all service dogs can do it. Some do tasks like get help if there's a problem or bring medicines or steady the person if they're feeling faint. But she's got that something extra." With a stretch, Isabeau's spine arched back, drawing his eye as she settled against the desk again. "There. I have all I need to order your new wardrobe. Some of it has to be special-ordered, but I can pick up what you'll need for your sister's wedding."

"Thanks, I appreciate it. But I hope you know that clothes aren't going to change the core of who I am or what I say."

There. He'd thrown down the gauntlet.

He'd enjoyed this fitting session a helluva lot more than he ever would have expected. And he knew without question that the woman in front of him had made all the difference in the day. Already he looked forward to their next sparring match.

So why not make the most of this month of jumping through social hoops?

His hand whispered against her impossibly soft skin, tension mounting as their eyes locked. "The best way to keep my rogue mouth in line is to stay right by my side. Be more than a media consultant. Be my date for my sister's wedding."

Two

When she'd been a kid, Isabeau, like other little girls, had dreamed of a fairy-tale wedding of her own. Her mother had even spun those fantasies with her. Except her mom's prince charming had walked out, and even though her mother kept telling the stories, Isabeau stopped believing. She wasn't sure she even knew what a healthy dating relationship was, between her mother's experiences and her own.

So how had she let herself get talked into being Trystan's date at a family wedding? She'd said yes before she could think, her mind somehow losing its edge around this man.

A dozen times over the past two days she'd planned to tell him it was a silly idea.

And every time, she'd found a reason to delay until here they were, together, at a Mikkelson-Steele wedding.

Sure it was a small ceremony at the Steele family compound by the water, but still. Simple to these people still involved big money and security guards.

She wasn't his date, not in the romantic sense. Although Trystan was playing it to the hilt, his arm draped over her shoulders as the bride and groom exchanged vows.

Trystan leaned closer, whispering against her ear, "Do you feel okay?"

"I'm fine, just fine," Isabeau insisted quickly, then caught herself up short. "Why would you ask that?"

"Your face is all scrunched."

"That's rude." The mutter eked out between her lips, which were lifted in a tight smile. Though to be completely honest, she could feel the vise grip of tension in her teeth and furrowed brow.

"My apologies." His voice was low, but the lilt to his tone was light. Teasing. "Your *gorgeous* face is all scrunched?"

"Better, slightly."

"We're at a wedding. Pretend you aren't checking your watch wondering how much longer until the reception, like the rest of us are."

"That's not true. I'm enjoying the view. The sun

just made me squint for a second," she lied through her teeth.

"Uh-huh, right." He laughed softly.

She had to confess, a summer shoreline wedding in Alaska with a mountain range backdrop was nothing less than stunning. She would have enjoyed herself if it weren't for the nerves in her stomach generated by the man beside her.

Distracting her.

The Steele estate loomed in the background, sprawling, like a cedar wood cabin on the scale of a manor house—these clients were beyond the caliber of any she'd had before. The home was nestled into the skinny pines and rugged landscape, the wildness of it all giving Isabeau a small sense of peace even with the mansion housing multiple suites for the Steele family when they were in town. The quarters for each sibling were much like luxurious condominiums. Glenna Mikkelson had even been living in her suite with Broderick for months.

Having their wedding here also made it an easier location for Jack Steele. The patriarch had only recently been given the okay to stop wearing his neck brace. He was a walking miracle, given he'd fractured two vertebrae in his neck. He'd survived the fall and the surgery that followed.

He was still an imposing figure, but pale, and she suspected he would be sitting for the duration of the reception. Likely only pride and grit kept him on his feet now. Actually, Jeannie Mikkelson appeared more stressed, worried and frazzled than he was, even with her mother-of-the-bride smile.

Isabeau glanced up at Trystan to see if he'd noticed his mother's strain. But no. His gaze slammed right into hers with a spark of awareness that made her all the more conscious of his arm along her shoulders.

Lord, he smelled good, like spices and musk and man.

He smiled, which distracted her to the point she almost missed Trystan's hand sliding down her spine to rest just above her butt. Her skin was on fire in a way she hadn't felt in a long—a very long—time.

Why was he doing this? To rebel against the makeover or because he genuinely wanted her? His behavior felt like more than playacting through a simple date. She would need to tread warily to resist getting too involved with him.

She cleared her throat and hissed, "Pay attention to your sister's wedding."

"Yes, ma'am." Trystan's hand eased upward to her shoulder again.

It had to be the wedding ceremony making her go all gooey inside, aching to grasp some of that magic in the air.

The wedding. Right. She should just pay attention to the proceedings, take in the staging and beauty for ideas for future clients who wanted a down-to-earth, simple ceremony.

The bride wore a fitted lace dress with long, sheer sleeves and a sculpted bodice, her blond hair swept up in a twist that exposed her regal neck. She held a bouquet of flowing Queen Anne's lace, white roses and greenery. Simple and elegant, like the bride herself.

The groom's tuxedo was a Ralph Lauren design with clean lines, and no Stetson today.

Unlike the other men, who all wore suits and hats.

The family resemblance on both sides was easy to spot. The Mikkelsons were blond or had hair a lighter shade of brown. The Steeles were dark haired like their father with a flash of Inuit heritage from their mother.

Isabeau had done her research on both families. The Mikkelson matriarch and Steele patriarch had both been devastated when their spouses died. She'd sifted through countless press releases to identify possible publicity pitfalls. But there were no hints of scandal in either of their marriages. It was impossible not to root for them now that they were planning their own wedding.

Glenna Mikkelson and Broderick Steele's relationship was a bit more…complicated. Rumors indicated they'd had a brief fling in college, but Glenna had gone on to marry someone else. Her husband had cheated and fathered a baby daughter with another woman—who had then abandoned her child.

The precious little girl was in Broderick's arms now, her chubby hands wrapped around his neck.

Isabeau's heart squeezed at the beauty of a real fairy-tale wedding. And with unerring timing, Trystan slid his hand down to palm her waist with a warm, subtle strength that sent tingles up her spine.

God, she needed some space from this sexy "date" of hers.

The chords of an upbeat song called her back, grounding her in the moment. Head tilting, she watched as the couple walked down the aisle together. Glenna glowed as she passed them, her smile as wide as the horizon and as brilliant as the midsummer sun. She lifted the baby up as Broderick led them all the way down the velvet aisle.

A family. Complete and ready to face the future together.

A chord in Isabeau's heart snapped as the wedding concluded.

Suddenly, the world seemed to close in on her. The small crowd felt oppressive.

Space. The desire to bolt surged into her rapidly beating heart. "You know, you're right after all about the reception. I'm starving." She gestured to the caterer's tent on the lawn. "I'm going to check out the spread while you chat with your family. Bye now."

She smoothed her silky yellow dress, the hem teasing her knees, and slipped out from beneath Trystan's arm. Her skin tingled with the lingering feel of his simple touch. Her heels sunk into the grass as she made her way up the hill toward the outdoor party tent. Tables of food were strategically available everywhere she looked, even up to the balcony and sunroom. Waiters walked the grounds with trays of canapés and drinks.

She didn't have her dog with her, opting to let Paige play with the other family dogs in a large fenced area. Isabeau had decided that if she changed her mind, she could retrieve Paige quickly. Even now, she could see her yellow Lab loping with a husky, each dog holding the end of a stick not even sparing a glance at the large antlered moose ambling just beyond the fence line.

Best smile forward, Isabeau dashed away from the amassing family, from Trystan's heat, her eyes trained on reaching the balcony.

Don't look back at him.

Determined to find a moment of solitude, Isabeau headed straight for the mansion, climbing the lengthy stairway up to the balcony. What a breathtaking view of the festivities. And yes, she could find peace here as well, away from the temptation of leaning into Trystan's touch.

An elegant, understated spread of high tables drenched in pale lace and lit candles filled the balcony. The candles flickered, contrasting with the deep blue depths of the water lapping against the shore below.

Navigating her way from the balcony to the sunroom, she paused to lean against one of the sunroom's many open doors. Pausing to drink in the scene. To collect herself and assuage the mounting anxiety that rumbled in her chest, squeezing around her heart.

Golden sunlight drenched the room, pouring through the array of windows. An ice carving of a doe and buck glimmered, drawing her toward the spread of food. Casting a glance at the lawn again, she saw the other guests beginning to help themselves to the alfresco meal, with the option of retreating to the sunroom. Thank goodness for the spread out space for mingling or quiet. Because she felt jittery and she knew it had nothing to do with her blood sugar levels.

Salmon, ahi tuna, crab legs, asparagus, Caprese skewers…all of it made her mouth water. She built a plate of salmon and a plain roll just as a jazz band inside the house launched into their first set.

Yep. Fairy tale. And yes, a part of her still wanted a moment of magic like this. Not the angst of forever. Just the magic.

With a sigh, some of the restlessness she'd felt only five minutes ago seemed to dissolve. Making her way outside, she sat on one of the deck chairs, scanning the surreal beauty in front of her.

Isabeau tipped her face toward the brief warmth of summer, four weeks in late June and early July. Temperatures in the fifties felt balmy after her first winter in the state.

And while the thought of such cool weather feeling balmy never ceased to amaze her, the wild scenery of this state made her feel humble and small. In her college literature class, she'd been forced to read Thoreau and Emerson. At the time, their musings on nature had washed over her in a blur of words. But here, as she studied the purple of dwarf fireweed peeking through exposed granite along the shoreline, the perceptiveness of those dusty American thinkers resonated. Even with the helicopter parked in the distance.

Serenity and peace.

Well, at least it had been for a few brief shining moments. Isabeau sat up straighter as Naomi Steele approached, her belly round with her second trimester pregnancy, her dark hair gathered into an elegant bun, teardrop emerald earrings nearly brushing her shoulders. Those Steele eyes sharp, but tired. Isabeau couldn't tell how far along Naomi was—guessing months or ages had never been her strong suit.

"Do you mind if I hide out here with you?" She rested a hand on her pregnant belly. "Royce is driving me crazy about how long I've been on my feet and if I don't sit and eat soon he's going to start hand-feeding me, which would be embarrassing."

"He sounds adorable." Isabeau had spent considerable time with all the family members this past week, but somehow Royce Miller had a way of making himself scarce if there were more than two other people in the room.

"Hmm… *Adorable* isn't a word I would choose.

He's sexy and brooding and a great guy. But he's also a worrier and I want to relax for a moment for some girl talk with my artichoke heart pizza—yes, I know pizza isn't normally at a reception but I have been craving it."

"I think it's delightful and actually have seen it showing up on a number of event menus." She tossed a smile over her shoulder at one of the Steele brothers as the room began to fill up.

Where was Trystan?

"And you won't rat me out about the three fruit tarts?"

Isabeau pretended to zip her mouth shut, a theatrical wink following. She leaned in to whisper, "My lips are sealed."

Naomi lifted one of the fruit tarts toward her lips, clearly excited to indulge. She popped the tart into her mouth, chewing thoughtfully. Moments passed before Naomi broke the silence, her eyes trained on the horizon. "We appreciate your help with Trystan. This merger means everything to us."

"You both have beautiful families."

"And we understand blending everyone into a congenial unit is about more than blending the businesses. But if meshing the companies doesn't go smoothly, we don't stand a chance."

"Trystan is being cooperative, which is more than I can say for some of my clients." She liked this family, both sides. Which made her feel all the more disloyal for her attraction to Trystan. She owed everyone her best effort.

"Probably because he thinks it's for only a month." Naomi folded her pizza slice in half and ate with an expression of bliss on her face.

"Pardon me?" Setting the plate down on her lap, Isabeau turned to face Naomi.

"The fund-raiser is in just less than a month, but I think everyone is hoping that some of your influence will last beyond that time and he'll be more involved. We would like all the siblings to be more involved, but I'm not sure that's going to happen, not with Trystan or some of the others, as well."

Isabeau looked over at the dance floor, at the other family members in question. Delaney, the quietest of the Steele siblings, fluffed her hair. She seemed to shrink into the background, her body language tense. Her younger teenage brother, Aiden, came up to her, dancing circles around her. A true goofball in the way only a teenager seemed to be able to get away with. The reception hall was filling up, only a few left in the sunroom.

Naomi cleared her throat, dropping her voice low as people began to pour through the sunroom into the reception area. "But really, you've done a great job with Trystan. It was evident today."

"Thank you. He's been very cooperative."

She glanced at Isabeau, grinning. "I bet he has."

Isabeau chose to ignore the insinuation. "This was

a nice chance to watch how he interacts and make notes of what to work on over the next few weeks."

"We're lucky to have you. Takes a lot of pressure off us." Naomi skimmed another touch across her pregnant stomach. Her long, slender face gazing downward, possibilities seemingly dancing before her dark brown eyes. A long sigh rippled through Naomi. "I had no idea when I decided to get pregnant through in vitro fertilization how upside down my family was about to be with the merger, my brother's wedding, my dad's engagement."

"Congratulations on the baby."

"I'm pregnant with *two* babies actually. I should have considered the possibility." A small silence echoed after those words. In a less aggressive, less confident voice, Naomi added, "I'm a twin."

Pain twisted in the woman's beautiful face, pulling at Isabeau's heart.

Isabeau touched the pregnant woman's arm, offering a small—hopefully welcome—sign of comfort. "Your sister who…?"

"Yes, my sister who died in the plane crash along with our mother."

"I'm so sorry."

"I wish I could say it gets easier to handle with time, but it only gets easier to hide the pain. I can't help but think of them today."

Isabeau nodded in agreement. "Of course, that's only natural."

"You're a very good listener. I never expected to talk about this tonight."

"I'm glad I could help."

"I should get back to my fiancé. He'll be chomping at the bit for me to sit down, put my feet up, eat something from every food group."

"That's sweet that he's so attentive." Jitters pelted her, along with memories of her college boyfriend. His attentiveness had turned into something ugly—controlling obsession. She didn't see that in Royce, but she understood too well the sensation of feeling smothered.

Naomi rolled her eyes. "A little too attentive. But I do love him." She pushed herself up from the chair. "I enjoyed chatting. Let's do this again."

Isabeau couldn't miss the way Naomi's face lit up when she spotted her fiancé. The way he returned her smile. There was so much love in the air here. Did these families understand how lucky they were?

Although she wasn't sure she could trust all this happiness if it landed on her doorstep with a bow.

Striding past a harpist playing on the lawn at the reception, Trystan scanned the wedding guests in search of Isabeau. Had she gone inside to the sunroom or great room? Even for a gathering of just family and friends went beyond what most would call an intimate affair.

His plan to bring Isabeau as his date had been

the perfect distraction from the way his family was meshing with the Steeles. His sister was marrying a Steele now. His mother would be marrying the Steele patriarch in a month.

The fact that his sister's wedding was at the Steele family compound rather than the Mikkelson home made him edgy and, yeah, angry too. As if the Steeles were working to erase all traces of the Mikkelsons.

All the more reason for him to make a success of this month as the face of their merged company.

That didn't mean he couldn't enjoy his time with Isabeau. No question, sparks were flying.

He had a sense that up until now, particularly in his interactions with women, he'd been sleepwalking, stumbling through the motions. But Isabeau jolted him, electrified his core.

Surprising him each time he saw her—like now.

He strode faster up the stairs to the deck leading to an enclosed sunroom. And damn, did she look hot today, sunlight catching the flames of red in her hair as she sat by herself in the sunroom, her legs delicately crossed. Manicured fingers gripped a now empty plate, traces of crumbs decorating the china.

A vision.

That's what she was. A vision he very much wanted to touch, hold and more, so much more. With the signature bravado that enabled him to approach even the flightiest and most aggressive horses, he drew in a breath and walked toward her with the Mikkelson swagger that had turned the onetime small business into an oil empire.

She sipped a glass of champagne, her bright eyes focusing on him as he drew closer.

"Come with me." Extending a hand, he noticed as her lips parted, brows raising in subdued—but visible—interest.

"Okay. You're the boss." She stared awkwardly at her plate, seeming unsure what to do with it.

Taking it from her, he set it down on a nearby table. She set her now empty champagne flute down too, rising to take his outstretched hand. "Where are we going?"

"Dancing," he said simply as they moved to the center of the great room. The small jazz band was tucked in the corner amidst the woodland themed decorations and a small space was cleared for dancing. So far the tunes had all been of the slower variety, and he hoped they stayed that way, eager for the feel of Isabeau against him.

"Dancing?" She laughed lightly, but still kept her soft hand tucked in his. "Now you've surprised me."

The band segued into a Sinatra classic and Trystan didn't miss a beat. He pulled her into his arms. He slipped his hand to her waist, letting it rest in the curve of her slender body. She seemed to lean into him, ever so slightly. Enough to send his blood pumping through his veins.

"I do know how. Mother insisted on lessons for all of us, everything from the basic ballroom styles to a session on square dancing."

"Good for Jeannie. Did you protest?" Her steps synched with his from the first move.

"Hell no, I was worried my family would get rid of me—" He stopped short. He didn't want to bust the mood here with talk about his insecurities during the early days when he'd been adopted. "Bad joke. I tend to blurt out what I'm thinking."

"Honesty is an admirable trait. It's just…" She bit her bottom lip.

A low laugh burst free. "Not always the most tactful for the business world."

A major part of why he was better cut out for his role managing the family ranch.

"That makes tact sound dishonest somehow."

Wanting to lighten the mood and chase away the shadows in her eyes, he twirled her away, the silky yellow dress fanning around her lithe legs. Radiant and sexy. She spun back to him, her hands finding his.

"I only meant that I get that there are nuances and things that are better left unsaid. I'm just not a nuance kind of man." Keeping her close, he guided their steps away from the other half-dozen couples dancing, steering her toward the stone fireplace. Massive moose antlers stared down at him. Tall ceilings provided an airy balance to the thick leather sofas that were now strategically staged against the walls rather than in their normal places.

"Let's talk about the dancing more. You're a natural. I think we should capitalize on that this month in your image building. This has a great sophisticated look to it. With the right press coverage—"

"Isabeau, seriously, the image again?" He needed a night off from all of that. The past week had been intense and outside his comfort zone. Particularly the past two days when all he could think about was having her here tonight. In his arms for a dance.

Yes, he wanted a night he could enjoy. With her.

"Could you stop with the business talk and let's just enjoy this dance?"

"Oh, um, sure. This must be an emotional day for you, with your sister getting married and your mom engaged—"

"Emotional?" He stifled a laugh, drawing her closer to his chest. He whispered against her ear, as they swayed in time to the music, "It's just a wedding. That's it. I'm focused on you."

"Wait, our being here together is supposed to be about business, working on your image."

He smiled, his blue eyes glinting.

She swatted his arm. "Stop that or I'm going to line up a dozen more press conferences for you."

"I didn't say a word so I couldn't have shoved my boot in my mouth."

"Your smile speaks volumes."

His grin widened.

"Trystan, that's not professional—or fair."

And perhaps that proclamation would have been followed by a moment—the kind he'd been thinking about nonstop since the day of the fitting—but a cacophony of voices disrupted the intensity of their eye contact, the closeness of their bodies.

Isabeau pivoted toward the noise first. Chuck and his wife, Shana, stood at the edge of the dance floor. Heat seemed to rise around them, calling a tempest into the room as their voices escalated, beginning to drown out the jazz tune.

His cousin, Sage Hammond, moved between them, her voice low and calming. While Trystan couldn't make out what the argument was about this time, it was clear that Sage was playing peacemaker. A role he'd seen his fierce butterfly of a cousin play on behalf of her aunt and boss, Jeannie Steele.

He felt Isabeau tense, clearly uncomfortable with a family altercation. Squeezing her hand, Trystan tilted his head and mouthed, "Follow me."

A quick nod of agreement was all the encouragement she needed to leave the tense scene unfolding nearby. He maneuvered them outside, taking the path to the boathouse on the bay, near the seaplane.

Toward a small section of the compound all their own.

Three

As the sounds of the spat faded, replaced by the light wind rustling through the low-hanging tree branches that gathered, sentry-like, at the left corner of the boathouse, Isabeau felt her heartbeat intensify.

Trystan's slightly calloused hand wrapped around hers. His skin, rough from ranch work—hands clearly used to the brush of leather reins—sending her own skin humming with awareness. She was drawn to the dichotomy of him, a tycoon in boots.

She hated to admit it, but part of her eagerness to escape his family's chaos had a lot to do with the draw of this man. In her line of work, she'd found herself frequently at the epicenter of familial disputes. It came with the territory of image curation.

But this felt different from her experience with any other client. Isabeau knew why too.

It had everything to do with the man with the charismatic, gruff demeanor.

She heard the distant bark of her dog and glanced over her shoulder to be sure Paige wasn't fretting about being away from her. A quick check assured her that her yellow Lab was still enjoying playtime with her new pals—a husky named Kota and a Saint Bernard named Tessie.

Isabeau turned her attention back to Trystan, surprised at the ease in her steps. She didn't feel the urgent need to have her dog close. A relaxed and mellow sensation flowed through her veins.

Along with a total awareness of this big, sexy man. An outdoorsman who danced with a confidence and smoothness that made her body burn.

And she couldn't help but glory in the feeling. So many of her panic attacks stemmed from negative encounters with men.

Some of the males who had flocked to her beautiful, weary mother had crowded Isabeau.

And then came her college boyfriend, who'd never laid a hand on her but stole her privacy by stalking her every move until she'd been forced to take out a restraining order.

People could leave a scar on a person's soul in so many ways.

Yet, something about Trystan put her at ease.

His total honesty.

He might be rough around the edges, but he was authentic and that kept her moving forward along with him. She would worry about the impropriety issue later. Right now, she could only think about how hot she'd found him since the first time she'd laid eyes on him.

Leading her inside, he flipped on the lights, the switch igniting the darkness in front of her with the warm glow of yellow-hued lamplight. Golden illumination revealed the luxury of even this aspect of the property.

Plush couches and well-appointed wooden furniture. A row of yellow two-person kayaks lined the wall farthest from them, complementing the neatly arranged fishing poles and nets. A powerboat docked in the water nearby, bobbing up and down, adjacent to a sitting area with Sedona-orange-colored cushions decorating a couch and two chairs. Waterproof, she realized, though they still seemed overstuffed…

Trystan turned a slow circle. "It's definitely quieter here."

She drew in a breath of the salt-laden air. "You did well at the wedding with the photo shoots."

There hadn't been media present, but still, he'd

put on his game face for the shots to be released to the press.

"So I've earned my respite from the masses?"

"Is that what this is? An escape, a break?" She smoothed her silky dress, her fingers—her senses—hyperaware of every texture down to the timbre of his whiskey-smooth voice.

His blue eyes lit with a smile. "Actually, this was about getting time alone to talk to you about something other than work. I think we've both earned that. Do you agree? Or is it back to business for us?"

"I do agree," she answered, wanting to linger in the mellowness between them a while longer.

"Good, good." He strode toward the refrigerator and opened it, surveying the contents. "Ahh… What have we here?"

He pulled out a bottle of beer bearing the Mikkelson family brewery label—Icecap. He glanced at Isabeau. "There's wine and water, as well."

Inclining his head, he suggested they make their way over to the sitting area.

"The beer sounds good, but the water is probably safer for me, with my diabetes, after everything I enjoyed at the reception." She eyed the deck of cards on the table suspiciously. "Why the cards?"

He dropped onto the sofa, his body relaxed. Open. Inviting, as he handed her the water bottle. Their hands brushed, a crackle passing between them.

A blush heated her face, warmth spreading further until her body tingled with awareness. She sipped the water, suddenly so very thirsty, then set it on the table alongside the two decks of cards.

"I'm not luring you here to play strip poker. Scout's honor. I'm still learning my way around the Steeles' home but Broderick invited me out here for one of their card games—and a drink. I guess this is a man cave of sorts." He tipped back a swig of his beer. "I got the impression you'd had enough of the crowds too."

"It has been a full day." She offered up the minimal concession.

She played down her anxiety. Always. Very few people knew how she suffered. For a painstaking moment, she wondered if there'd been a hint of her discomfort today—the very thing she labored to hide. A small well of anxiety bubbled in her stomach at the thought, the reality of her condition threatening to break loose. She found herself reaching for her dog only to remember she'd left Paige out playing with the husky and Saint Bernard.

One steadying breath settled her nerves and she decided to stay put rather than bolt.

"So, Isabeau, what made you choose this line of work?" His sky blue eyes narrowed as he leaned forward, his knee just bumping hers.

Her heart hammered, the musky scent of him teasing her every breath. She spoke, even as she found her gaze locked with his, unable to look away.

"I have a degree in marketing and public relations. I did some work in the media world, even reporting for a while, but found I'm more comfortable behind the scenes."

"I bet the cameras loved you."

"Thank you for the compliment." She reached for her water bottle, the condensation seeming to cool her down, to give her a sense of stability even though another part of her wondered what his lips tasted like. She avoided his eyes, hesitant to bring up the real reason she hid from cameras while encouraging others to overcome their own anxieties.

"You're welcome. What do you mean by 'more comfortable' behind the scenes?"

"I feel more in control." And Isabeau did everything possible to give herself the trappings of control. Well-organized lists, binders, schedules. Anything that gave structure to an otherwise chaotic world. She'd needed those tools after her father left and her mother struggled to keep a roof over their heads. Then her anxiety had ramped up all the more when her college boyfriend decided breaking up wasn't an option.

"Nerves?"

"You could say that." She pushed aside thoughts of the past, unwilling to have that time in her life steal anything more from her. "I believe in some ways my anxiety makes me more empathetic to the people I'm hired to help as they search for an approach to fame that fits them."

"Interesting viewpoint."

She scratched a fingernail along the bottle. "I'm happy to help you, but you seem to have nearly a perfect life, and a good amount of family support around you."

His normally assured smile fell, replaced by pain that crinkled in the edges of his eyes, the corners of his mouth. In a tight voice, his gaze too focused on the label of the bottle, he said, "No life is perfect. We all have plans, regrets, hopes."

A strain in her heart answered. She had to touch his hand. "What are your plans and hopes for the future?"

"You mean like a bucket list?"

"Sure."

"How about you start?"

"Okay." She drummed her fingers along the bottle, thinking. "I want to learn a new language. It will help me with my business."

"Pick up an instrument. My siblings play, but by the time I joined the family I was past those early years when kids usually start music lessons."

"It's not too late." She found herself warming to this topic, to sharing hopes with him, the world narrowing to just the two of them. "What about the guitar?"

"Maybe. But it's your turn..." He draped an

arm along the back of the sofa, his skin brushing her shoulder, crackling the static in the air all over again.

Except she knew full well it wasn't static snapping through her veins. Not that she could bring herself to pull away. "I want to learn archery."

"Archery?" He picked up a lock of her hair.

She shrugged, thinking back to her love affair with the golden age of Hollywood, scenes of *Robin Hood* and *Ivanhoe* flooding her imagination. "It seems romantic."

"What about a crossbow?"

She scrunched her nose, then relaxed. "Not for me, but it could be hot if it's a guy using it."

He chuckled, low and husky. "Well, that's a distracting notion." He tugged the lock of her hair gently. "What about your bucket list?"

There were so many things. So many things she wanted for her life. So many things she felt were out of her grasp because of her anxiety.

She released a deep exhale with the words as they took on the power of a flash flood. "Whale watching. Stomping grapes in Italy. Speaking in front of people. Riding a camel."

"Whoa, back up." He lifted a hand.

"Grapes. I know. Unexpected." She clinked her bottle to his.

"I was focused more on the part about talking in front of a group. That's surprising, given your job." He stroked the side of her face, his hand then gravitating back to that loose lock of hair.

"I know what should be said and done. I just choke if I'm the one having to say it. So I teach others."

He simply nodded, leaving her words there, giving her space—which somehow managed to draw her closer because he understood her. No judgment in his eyes.

She'd never known that peace and fire could co-exist, but here, now, the two twined into an intoxicating blend. That, along with the whole fairy-tale day, sent her swaying toward him.

The thin sliver of space between them heated with their breaths. He lifted one hand, sketching the backs of his knuckles along her cheekbone. Her pulse quickened, her body tingling, and she tipped her head into his caress.

She swallowed, holding his gaze. Feeling the air become heavy with awareness until—yes—her lips found his. That spark exploded as she tasted him.

His hands felt like magic gliding down her back, the silk of her dress caressing her skin along with each stroke of his fingers.

With a whispery moan, she angled closer to him, the warm wall of his body a perfect fit against her. He deepened the kiss, his hold both strong and careful, the taste of him delicious. Her thoughts scrambled as Trystan's touch drove her need higher, made her want more.

Want everything.

There was something about weddings that just made people do crazy, impulsive things. All that emotion running high with the promise of lifelong happiness.

Apparently she wasn't immune.

She'd noted the effect of weddings on others more times than she could count during her early days as a wedding planner. Bridesmaids and grooms-men hooked up after their walk down the aisle, as if that moment had somehow made them yearn for marriage. Those feelings usually faded for at least one of the people, once endorphins from the or-gasm waned.

Married couples who arrived at the event bicker-ing and plucking at their formal wear soon got that nostalgic look in their eyes.

Others just got drunk and stupid.

Isabeau wasn't sure what category she fell into.

None of them seemed to quite fit. But here she was, in the boathouse with Trystan Mikkelson, desire firing through her veins, both of them ditching their essential clothing. Her panties. His pants unzipped and inched down. Their legs tangled as they backed toward a wall-long bench covered in a blue canvas cushion with cute white anchors woven into the pattern. What a strange detail to notice, but all her senses were in hyperdrive.

Slim stripes of light slanted through the vents along the ceiling. The window was sealed tight and shuttered. The door closed. The dim lighting added to the anonymity of the impulsive moment.

She knew better.

And right now couldn't find the will to care.

She just wanted this man. Here. Now. And yes, maybe part of that wanting was a mourning for the future she couldn't bring herself to hope for— home, family, kids.

Her trust had been too damaged when she was too young.

Perhaps that's why this sexy cowboy oil mogul appealed to her. He was a lone wolf. A man more at ease away from people. He didn't need her and made his lack of concern about getting married very clear. He was content to leave propagating to all his other siblings.

So she could indulge in some of that wedding event magic for tonight.

Her soft skin made him ache to touch more of her, but the chill in the air meant it was unwise to ditch all their clothes—not to mention there were dozens of people outside partying beyond the locked door.

He hadn't expected things to go so far between

them, but damn if he could bring himself to stop. She'd lit a fire in him since she'd touched him during that simple clothes fitting.

Simple?

Nothing with this woman was simple. She was a complex blend of bold and reserved, poised but with a wildness to the intense grip of her fingers sliding under his shirt, her nails scoring along his back.

Her passion seared him.

She shook her shoes free and they thudded to the floor. She sketched her foot along his calf, her legs gliding higher.

No question, this was escalating fast. "Are you sure this is what you want?"

"Trust me. I want. Oh so much." She pushed aside his suit coat.

"We can find somewhere less rustic." He slid his hand up her dress to her low-cut panties, simple strings along each hip holding the satin together.

"That would mean waiting and I am one hundred percent against waiting." She loosened and freed his tie.

Her voice was husky but sure. A very, very good thing. Persuading her to be his date to a wedding had been a good idea after all, a plan that was going to lead to a much more pleasurable month than he'd originally expected.

"My wallet."

"What?" Her hands paused along his suit pants.

"Get my wallet from inside my jacket. Condom."

"Oh. Right." With a speed and deftness he applauded, she fished out his wallet, found a condom and tossed his billfold on the floor.

Sheathed and very much ready, he stroked up her thigh and settled between her legs. Her soft arms looped around his neck and rational thought fled, replaced with a frenetic chemistry. Pleasure. Perfection. A coupling he hadn't even known was on his bucket list.

But now he knew he couldn't imagine having missed this moment with Isabeau.

And damn, but she was eager and more confident than he'd expected. She guided him and then… His mind was a blur of sensation and movement and this woman. This fluid goddess of a woman in his arms. So elegant and yet totally at ease in this earthly boathouse.

His heart pounded in his ears in time with their bodies moving against each other like the lap of the water against the dock, the roll of the waves. Her breathing hitched faster with little gasps as she urged him on, close already and sounding so earnest and honest. Her hands slid into his pants, her nails digging into his hips.

And just when he thought he couldn't hold back any longer, her back arched upward, her soft breasts pressing against his chest and reminding him he had so much more of her to explore when they made love again.

And there would be more, damn it.

The thought sent his release slamming through him like a wave crashing free from under an iceberg. His arms clenched around her tighter as they rolled to their side, aftershocks rippling through them both.

The end of their lovemaking came in the form of ragged breaths growing steady. Quietness descended in the boathouse, despite the roaring elements of the wedding band filtering through the air. He gathered her close, noting the light scent of her perfume as he stroked her hair, fingers trailing down her shoulder.

Trystan could feel her heartbeat rattling in her chest as she leaned against him. Half-dressed, he wanted to keep this moment going. The taste of the chemistry leaving him intrigued—determined.

Isabeau moved slightly, and in the din of half-formed melodies…she winced against him. "Ouch!" she exclaimed softly.

He shifted up on one elbow, looking down at her pained face. "Ah hell, what's wrong? Did I hurt you? The last thing I wanted to—"

"Charley horse." The throw blanket clasped to her, she sat up, curled over and rubbed her leg. "In my calf. Ouch, ouch, ouch—it's so fierce."

He reached for her, and she pulled back, but he

insisted, cupping her calf and massaging along the tensed muscle. "I want to help."

Blanket clutched to her chest, she flopped back, surrendering her leg. "I'm embarrassed enough already. Just let me deal with this on my own. I'll be fine in a minute."

He soaked up the feel of her and searched for some of his newfound verbal skills. He needed to convince her to give them a second chance to be together like this. "Really, let me. It's no different than rubbing a real horse."

Horse? Hell. So much for the new, suave speaking skills.

"Did you seriously just compare me to a horse? I'm not feeling very complimented."

"Poor choice of words. You're sexy as hell." He swept his eyes over her, taking in her flushed cheeks and loose, tousled hair. "You don't need me to tell you that. You need me to help you bear weight on that leg without screaming so loudly you bring the whole wedding party in here."

"Oh, good point. We're seriously underdressed for that kind of group get-together."

"What an understatement." He kissed the freckles along her collarbone, savoring the patch of satiny skin.

"Somehow, we've turned this into more than just a date. And a date was all we agreed to."

He palmed her back and brought her closer. "Is

there a rule against us following where the mood took us?"

"No, not specifically." Her freckled nose twitched contemplatively. "But what just happened could make our working relationship sticky if things go badly."

"And what if things don't go badly?"

Her eyelids fluttered shut, and she seemed to gather her thoughts. Eyes back open, she moved away from him, hands seeking her scattered clothes. "Emotions can cloud judgment. I pride myself on my professional reputation."

"I can understand that."

"I'm embarrassed."

"Don't be." He swept a hand over her auburn hair.

"We can't let it happen again."

"How about we cut a deal?" He started buttoning his shirt. "I'll keep my hands to myself for the next thirty days while you're on the payroll."

"Thank you." She knelt on the ground, searching for her shoes under the sofa.

"But I want to make it clear, that doesn't mean I'll stop trying to get you to ask me to put my hands on you." He started to zip his pants, and…

"You have to realize I don't want anyone to know about this. In fact, as I just said, it can't happen again." She put on one shoe, then the other. "It's unprofessional, not to mention distracting from what we need to accomplish. And it's not like this fling would be going anywhere."

Hell. He reached for her arm. "Isabeau—"

"Don't get me wrong, it was great sex and I don't regret it. We just need to make a pact that this is what it is—a wedding hookup."

He repeated, "Isabeau—"

"What?"

There was no easy way to say this. "You may want to rethink our acting like mere work acquaintances. It could be helpful to the cause."

"Thanks, but no."

He eased her back to sit beside him, holding her eyes with his. "Being a couple would make things easier if we have news to deal with a month from now."

"News to deal with? I'm sorry, but I'm not following you."

"Isabeau, the condom broke."

Four

The afterglow of awesome lovemaking faded fast.

"What did you say?" Isabeau prayed she'd heard wrong.

Surely she had. Even though she knew full well exactly what he'd said. She willed back the tide of panic.

"The condom broke," he repeated, zipping his pants and exhaling. Hard. "I am so damn sorry. But I want you to know that if there's a baby, I will take care of both you and the child—"

"Whoa, cowboy." She held up a hand to stop him. She could barely wrap her brain around the possibility of pregnancy. No way was she ready to leap into the future just yet. A future she really, really hoped didn't happen. "Slow your roll there. I'm still catching my breath and you're already planning for a future that's unlikely anyhow."

Sinking sunlight seemed to evaporate the warmth of the sunny Alaskan day. A chilling cold worked through the room, causing the hairs on the back of Isabeau's neck to stand on end, nerves working to form knots in her stomach. In the approaching dusk, the dull yellow lamplight provided minimal visibility.

"Unlikely? Famous last words." He shook his head. "We need to be prepared. I'm simply making sure you don't spend the next few weeks in limbo wondering where I stand."

Her panic level upped a notch at the thought of pushing this subject now, before she'd had a chance to process what she'd done with him…and what had happened. "Is that a pointed statement to nudge for information on where I stand?"

She fidgeted with her still-discarded dress, the talk of a nebulous future with a child she shared with this man feeling a bit like a hazed dream. The chilling night air seemed to grow more aggressive, and she yanked her dress on, letting the fabric wrap against her skin, providing warmth.

And a much-needed barrier.

He tucked her hair behind her ear gently. "If you're feeling so inclined."

The quality of light from the small table lamps no longer felt like enough. As if sensing her thoughts, he flicked on another switch, the bright overhead fluorescent fixture coming to life with a low hum.

"I'm not. Yet." She swallowed back more of that panic. Her last serious relationship had turned out to be with a possessive stalker. The thought of commitment made her throat start to close up. She wished she had her dog but she'd been overly confident, distracted.

Breathe—slow, deep breaths, no hyperventilating.

If she was pregnant, that limited her anxiety medication options. Oh crap. Just the thought made her heart pound harder. "When I have my head together, I'll let you know."

"Fair enough." His hand glided down between her shoulder blades. "How about we—"

"Not a chance. I may not know a lot of things right now, but I am absolutely certain we are not sleeping together again."

He pulled his hand back, raising both. "I was actually going to suggest we plan a time to talk away from here. But what is your reason for being so certain?"

Forcing herself to stand on wobbly legs, she smoothed her dress back down. Step one. Control her image. Small routines for this chaotic moment. Checking that her earrings were still in place, she turned to face him, drawing in a breath, trying to look more confident than she actually felt.

This had been such a mistake and she needed

to get out of here fast to sort through her thoughts with a clear head.

She chewed her bottom lip, then said carefully, "I'm sorry for presuming. You're right that we need to talk. This was impulsive and we both got caught up in the whole wedding aura cliché. It was a mistake, professionally and personally. And if—" she drew in a shaky breath "—there's a baby, then that's all the more reason for us to have already established an uncomplicated relationship."

"You think it's that simple? Decide to ignore the attraction and it will evaporate? I'm a man of the land and nature, and I have to disagree with your take on biology."

"You can disagree all day long but that won't change my stance." She pulled her spine straight, her hand trailing up to her hair. Practiced hands smoothed the strands that fell loose, which helped her sift through to one immutable fact. "From this point on, we have a business relationship only. The question of pregnancy will be answered by the time we attend the fund-raiser, and if the odds play out that there's no baby, we can part ways once and for all."

Night air whipped around Trystan, chilling him in a way it shouldn't for this time of year.

To say his mind was reeling would be the ultimate understatement. He leaned on a dock post, watching Isabeau disappear up the hill, her red hair perfectly rearranged as if nothing had happened between them.

The problem was that everything had happened between them.

Her curvy silhouette brought his memory back to the softness of her lips, the way she felt pressed against him. Beautiful. Stunning. Hot. Sex that made him lose his mind, forget his sensibilities. The kind that had him thinking of making this a long-term affair.

And all that had changed with a broken condom and Isabeau's retreat.

He also couldn't escape the unsettling possibility that she might be pregnant. He would live up to his responsibility. He would even offer to marry her if he thought there was a chance in hell she would say yes.

Her current level of horror at furthering their connection and her emphatic insistence on a business-only relationship indicated a marriage proposal would not be at all welcome.

He put a mental pin in the marriage proposal idea, tucking it aside for later consideration. He would never bail on his child like his biological parents had bailed on him. Any child of his would know he or she was wanted by both parents.

Royce Miller, Naomi's scientist fiancé, ambled toward him, the shirt beneath his suit jacket slightly disheveled. Royce, a quiet guy, always seemed lost in thought. Probably figuring out a math equation in his head that would revolutionize oil production, Trystan thought. No denying it—the man was a genius.

Royce drew up alongside Trystan. "Have you seen Naomi?"

"No, I haven't seen my future stepsister. But if I do, I'll let her know you're looking for her." Trystan adjusted his Stetson, turning back toward the water. Lights from the Steele compound reflected along the glassy surface.

Royce leaned against the dock railing, his cowboy hat dipping forward as he shook his head, his expression taut. "Better not put it that way. I'm trying to get her to take a breather and put her feet up. She's having none of that."

"She's an independent one."

Pacing, Royce appeared frazzled, like a tree rustling in a gust of wind. He moved toward the grass and knelt to examine a small rock. "An independent pregnant woman who doesn't seem to realize her ankles were really swollen last time I saw her."

Naomi's fiancé moved back to the rail, leaned against it, rock in hand.

Trystan shot him a look. "Probably not wise to lead with that when you find her. I'm no Romeo, but I'm guessing insulting a woman's water retention won't go over well."

Thumbing the rock over and over in his palm,

Royce nodded. "I'm aware. She's prickly as hell about being pampered. She's a confusing woman."

"Aren't they all?" Trystan's thoughts drifted away.

His question was more about Isabeau's potential pregnancy than about Naomi Steele's fiery independence.

As the company's temporary figurehead, an unplanned pregnancy with Isabeau could be a media nightmare. The irony was not lost on him that it was Isabeau who'd been specifically hired to curate his image. A much harder job if she became the epicenter of the crisis.

Damn. What would the next month look like? More important, what would the next eighteen years be like bringing up a child together?

"Do you have any advice for the next few weeks as I march around as the figurehead of this new company?"

With a flick of his hand, Royce skipped the rock. It skidded across the water for five beats before it plummeted into the depths with a defiant splash. "Why are you asking me?"

"You'll be a part of the family when you marry Naomi. Your role at the wilderness preservation wine and dine fund-raiser has been valued so far."

"You could ask Delaney."

Narrowing his eyes, Trystan shook his head dismissively. "You still have an outsider feel."

Something he identified with more than he was comfortable saying.

Royce shrugged, his attention already shifting back to the house. Likely thinking about his pregnant fiancée. "I'm not really family."

And at that, he turned to leave with an absent wave.

A deep pit formed in Trystan's stomach, sinking faster than the last rays of sunlight. "Neither am I."

Naomi eased out of her shoes, feet swollen and aching. She felt like an idiot for thinking she could pull off wearing a pair of heels to her brother's wedding.

For the few hours of the ceremony and reception, it had felt a bit like she'd stepped back in time. Back before she'd gotten pregnant, before she'd started a relationship with a sexy scientist who thrived in seclusion.

She and Royce had recently moved to a cabin on the outskirts of town. Remote. Romantic. Cozy.

Cozy was a fancy spin on the suffocation she'd been feeling lately.

It made sense to stay here tonight rather than driving an hour back to their little hideaway—longer if the weather acted up. She'd known the wedding would tax her stamina. She'd underestimated just how much it would though.

As she stepped out of the mansion's elevator, the motion sensor lights popped on, illuminating her room, recalling her old life. She breathed in deeply, reveling in the calm. Four months ago, Royce had blasted into her world. Or rather, she'd half conned her way into his. Pregnant with twins and trying to land the world's top oil industry engineer for fledging Alaska Oil Barons, Inc.

Safe to say, she'd accomplished more than that. Royce was a wonderful man.

His attention to her every whim and movement though was more than a little suffocating sometimes.

She couldn't help but wonder if he stayed with her and took such good care of her because he couldn't live without her—or because he needed to care for her and her babies the way he couldn't for the child he lost years ago? Were they a replacement?

Naomi tossed her shoes aside and pressed her hands to her aching back. Pregnancy exhaustion felt different from other types of tired. She wanted to voice her fears, but couldn't. If she did, Royce would tell her not to worry and have her wrapped in cotton in under sixty seconds flat.

With a sigh, she stood back up, making her way into the kitchenette area, rummaging through the still-well-stocked fridge for a water bottle. Thirst gnawed at her throat, her lips dry. Staying hydrated took extra effort lately.

She pulled out a cool water bottle, first pressing it into the nape of her neck. She cupped her belly, her smile spreading way past her face to fill her heart.

She really should start picking up nursery items for her suite here as well as their cabin. At least a couple of portable cribs set up to capture the sunshine.

During the day, her loft didn't need any artificial light. Huge windows allowed the Alaskan sun to poke through, permeating the living area.

Her swollen feet sunk into the softness of the Inuit rugs—gifts from her grandmother when she'd gotten her first college apartment, another cherished touch in this space.

From the rough-hewn beams on a slanted, arched ceiling hung a crystal chandelier that sent prisms dancing on the cream-colored sofa, brightening the quarters.

Water bottle in hand, Naomi made her way to the sunroom—her former sanctuary, relaxing onto the reclining sofa at the center of the temperature-controlled room. A dance of vibrant oranges and reds soaked the mountains, casting the landscape in a fiery blaze.

The distinctive whoosh of the elevator door interrupted her wandering thoughts.

Royce.

She glanced over her shoulder just as he cleared the French doors to the balcony. His brown eyes warmed as he met her gaze, like melted chocolate seeping over her.

Yeah, food was pretty much her go-to imagery for every thought these days.

His charisma reached her before he even skimmed a kiss on her neck, the sensitive patch warming, launching a tingle throughout her. He was so much more than his broodingly handsome good looks. His appeal was more than a leanly muscled body, broad shoulders. And yeah, he got bonus points for the thick dark hair a hint too long, like he'd forgotten to get a haircut, tousled like he'd just gotten out of bed.

All enticing. Sure.

But it was his eyes that held her.

Those windows to the soul. To the man. A man with razor-sharp intelligence in his deep brown gaze that pierced straight to the core of her and seemed to say, *Bring it woman. I can keep up.*

Every time she was near him, raw sexual attraction crackled so hot in the air she half expected icicles to start melting off the trees. If only the rest of their relationship was as simple.

Naomi extended a hand to him. "What took you so long? I've missed you."

"I was speaking with Trystan, looking for you." Royce angled down to kiss her.

"The Mikkelsons," she said wryly. "I never thought we would be tangled up with that family two times over through siblings and parents."

"It's been a surreal few months, that's for sure. Although there are so many people in both of your

families, surely the odds dictate a crossing of paths."
Settling into the end of the recliner, he followed her
gaze out to the scenery, the sinking rays. "I trust this
guy. I really think you can relax and take it easy."

"Yeah, right. Another excuse to get me to rest.
I'm going stir-crazy." She rolled her eyes.

"You're doing important work." He placed his
hand on her stomach tenderly.

God, he made her feel cherished. Even so, there
was a part of her insecure with what their relationship had become.

She didn't regret her decision to go the in vitro
route a couple of months before she'd met Royce.
Her babies were already a reality nestled firmly
in her heart. But she also wondered what it might
have been like if he and she had made these children together.

And then those doubts blindsided her again. She
wondered if he needed these babies to fill the place
in his heart left bare by the loss of his own child.
Did he need them more than he needed her?

As she searched his dark eyes, she reminded herself he was an innately honorable man.

And a very protective man.

"I can still think and be an active part of the family business. They need my legal advice."

"No one's saying you shouldn't consult."

She snorted.

He lifted her feet and placed them in his lap.

Practiced, patient hands worked in concentric massaging circles, pushing into the arches. "You're carrying twins. That already makes this a high-risk pregnancy. Think of our children."

"I resent the implication that I'm not."

No amount of rubbing could undo the insinuation that she would ever put her babies at risk. Her simmering temper flared, that courtroom no-nonsense edge pushing against her tongue.

"I wasn't implying anything."

"Don't back down just because you're worried my tender feelings will somehow compromise my health."

He stroked up through her calves, releasing layers of tension.

Damn. He made it so hard to be mad. Or stay mad. The pain in her aching legs melted.

"Naomi, I was reading some articles about high blood pressure—"

"My blood pressure is fine. Excellent in fact. Thanks for worrying though." Her words came out breathy as her body warmed under his caress.

"And we're going to keep it that way."

He knew exactly how to touch her, knew what her body needed. What it craved.

"Does that mean you won't make love to me even though the doctor says it's okay?" She grinned, looking at him through her eyelashes.

"It just means we'll do so very, very slowly..."
His roguish smile was unmistakable.

Strong arms reached around her, and Royce
scooped her against his chest, into a feeling of weight-
lessness she welcomed in these days of feeling more
than her normal self.

Doubts that had circled her earlier seemed to
slip from the forefront, becoming less intrusive as
he carried her into the suite, those dark eyes still
dancing as his gaze skimmed over her.

This.

This moment made her fears about his over-
protective nature and reclusive ways feel inconse-
quential.

Yes. She was all too willing to lose herself in
this moment.

Their relationship was still new, only a few months
old, a passionate explosion. They would sort through
the rest with time.

Because what they had was too precious to lose.

Since starting her consulting business four years
ago, Isabeau had met clients in their homes for a
variety of reasons. Despite her anxiety, those meetings didn't faze her. There'd always been a sense
of comfort, partly because her clients felt at ease
in their own spaces and it made the work of image
curation easier.

But not all clients were Trystan.

Drop-dead sexy Trystan with his newly clipped dark brown hair and sexy, steamy eyes. Isabeau had started to get used to her trips to Trystan's temporary office space for further consultation and make-over advice. The trips to his remote home had been scheduled in advance—standard really, but when making the schedule, she hadn't taken into account an impulsive hookup and a broken condom.

Her stomach plummeted a bit as she stared out the window of the seaplane. Smaller planes made flying feel more real, more adventurous, as she studied the landscape below, from the rocky shoreline to mountaintops that still carried a hint of snow even in summer.

That sense of adventure blended with an awareness of being in a small cabin space with a man she'd slept with, in a boathouse no less. A man who was her client.

A man she could not push from her thoughts no matter how hard she tried.

The events of yesterday's wedding brimmed in her mind, overflowing until her body hummed with the desire to repeat their boathouse encounter, but slower. And without a broken condom.

Nerves pattered in her stomach. She drew in one deep breath after another. If she was pregnant, she would handle it. She would love her child and provide a stable home. Thanks to the sacrifices her own mother had made, she had an education and a career on the rise. A surprise pregnancy would slow her down, but she wouldn't let it stop her.

She pushed aside whispers of fear. If the delicate balance of her diabetes flared out of control… No. She would be okay. She'd asked her doctor in the past and it could be managed.

She was in control.

Well, of everything except her feelings for the man beside her.

Trystan guided the Mikkelsons' tiny seaplane housing just the two of them, plus Paige who curled in a tight ball between Isabeau's seat and his. The dog's head rested against Isabeau's foot. She reached down to scratch the pup's ears, flopping them back and forth, taking comfort in the sensation.

She reminded herself of her plan to get through the next few weeks of this job with Trystan—until she knew where she stood.

Stay calm and keep your hands to yourself.

And above all, do not risk another broken con-dom.

Trystan shot a glance her way. "What made you choose the name Paige for your dog rather than something like Fluffy or Old Yeller?"

Talking about the tasks her dog performed still made her feel uncomfortable. She was learning to draw boundaries around what she shared, but it had been quite a process over the past year since she'd been partnered with a working dog. She'd always struggled with anxiety, which spiked her blood sugar. But she'd managed with medication and some counseling. But after the stalking incident, her life had spun out of control—as had her health. She'd needed more help, help that had come in a surprising four-legged package.

"Um, why are you curious about her name?"

"We put a lot of thought into naming our horses. I've found there's usually a clue to the individual's personality when I hear the story about why they chose the name."

"That's very insightful of you."

"You sound surprised. Should I be insulted?" He half teased, eyes steady on the controls. Alert. Aware.

Sexy as hell.

He commanded a cool confidence as he guided the plane through the clear sky.

"I apologize for not thinking before I spoke. But I guess now I have to be honest. You seem too... brusque." Sliding her gaze away from him, she peered out the window, down to the Alaskan topography. Lakes appeared like constellations among the green valleys, the lush color a brief but vibrant treasure in Alaska.

"Maybe I'm churning around some deep contemplation during all those quiet moments." He offered her a tight smile, and though his aviator sunglasses hid his eyes, she imagined they had a dash of mischief in them.

"Perhaps you are. I should know better than to prejudge."

"So, the name Paige?"

Tucking her feet beneath her, she turned in her seat. Inspired by the conversation. By the willingness to open up. She needed him to do that if she was going to turn him into the perfect mouthpiece of the company. "How about a trade? I'll tell you more about Paige if you'll tell me the story behind one of your horse's names."

"Fair enough." He nodded once, keeping his gaze forward. "I assume from the tone of your voice, I'm supposed to go first."

"That would be nice."

"You're tougher than you appear, by the way."

"Thanks. Your horse?" Leaning forward, she awaited his answer. Probably something gruff and manly. Perhaps named for a skill or attribute. Like Rocky.

"Jerome."

She laughed, then bit her lip. Not what she'd expected at all. "Seriously? Jerome?"

"Absolutely serious. I named my first horse Jerome."

Curiosity nipped as she pictured him as a child naming a horse such a serious name. "How old were you?"

"Eleven."

Scratching along her hairline, she frowned. "You got your first horse at eleven? I assumed in your family you would have started riding much younger."

"I did ride earlier—as a guest." He touched the back of his neck, his jaw tense. "I'm an adopted Mikkelson. I visited when I was younger but didn't live with them until they took me in officially."

He'd mentioned something like that before, but somehow this full revelation caught her unaware. "That's nowhere in your bio."

"I'm a cousin, actually. My biological mother and Jeannie are sisters. I spent a lot of time with the Mikkelsons growing up, when my parents would disappear. When I was eleven, they got divorced. My mother was going to put me into foster care. My aunt—Jeannie—stepped in and adopted me."

"That had to be such a hurtful, confusing time for you. I'm sorry."

"I was—am—lucky. Things could have turned out much worse for me. I've led a privileged life. I owe the Mikkelsons more than I can ever repay."

Realization dawned. "And that's why you're working so hard to help the company."

"The business means the world to them."

Silence fell between them, thick and heavy as Alaska snow. Every bit as chilly too.

"And the reason you named that first horse Jerome?"

"That first week I was at the Mikkelson place, the week my parents made it clear they weren't coming back this time—my biological father took a job in Australia and my mother didn't want to parent alone. Anyhow, my uncle gave me a young Tennessee walker horse and had me choose the name. I picked Jerome, the patron saint of orphans."

His words touched her heart, shifting her image of him ever so slightly. "Trystan, I'm—"

"No sympathy. Now your turn. Tell me the story behind your dog's name?"

After what he'd shared, she was almost embarrassed to explain how her dog was named. "I feel like I'm coming up short. My story isn't anywhere near as insightful as yours."

"Tell me anyway and let me be the judge." His voice held that teasing tone again that smoothed the edges of his gravelly timbre.

"Paige was named at the training facility. She came there as a puppy and spent two years learning the skills to be a service dog. The organization has a fund-raiser where people make a large donation to the group in exchange for naming rights to a puppy. Paige was named from a collection by a church youth group who wanted to honor one of their classmates who died in a car wreck."

"That's very moving…"

"Those donations make the service dogs more affordable for people who don't have the twenty to thirty thousand dollars it takes to complete the training."

"Two years of training?"

She nodded, lifting a hand to block the light of the sun. "Training, feeding, vetting by paid professionals, who also rely on assistance from volunteers. Paige started learning all the basics and then over time the staff saw where she would fit best. Once a dog 'graduates,' he or she is paired with an applicant who best matches the dog's skill set."

"And they know a dog's potential even from when they're a puppy?"

Her nerves eased as she settled into explaining the more factual aspects of a service dog. Facts were so much easier than emotions. Facts could ground her.

"Different groups work in different ways, but usually groups either know the lineage of the dogs or it's a dog under two years old that has had extensive temperament and health testing. A dog can still wash out of training for any number of reasons."

"What happens to those dogs?" He guided the plane to the right with a smooth turn of the yoke, the wing outside her window dipping ever so slightly.

"Sometimes there's another type of task they can do. And if not, the dog goes up for public adoption. The waiting list for those dogs is usually long."

"I had no idea so much went into it. I thought you trained too."

"I did have to go to training classes, and I go to brush-up classes, as well."

"I'm impressed by the whole process."

She looked down at Paige. The yellow Lab raised her head, those wide, brown, knowing eyes staring straight into her soul. Life without Paige…an impossible thought now. Tears pulled at her, a knot in her throat almost obscuring her words. "Thank you, but it's a huge help to have her in my life. I'm very lucky we were partnered up."

Silence came again, less oppressive than before. Not quite comfortable though.

The skyline began to reveal more pronounced dips in the Alaskan topography. Enchanting to take in from this perspective. Almost as mesmerizing as the man beside her.

Turning to glance at him, she noticed the furrow in his brow, fine lines digging deep.

Her stomach dipped with a sense of foreboding she could not shake.

"I hadn't thought about it until now—" Trystan leveled a glance at her over the top of his aviators, his eyes full of concern "—but how does your diabetes play into possible health problems if you're pregnant?"

Five

Trystan steered his Range Rover along the winding drive through the trees toward his ranch home.

He intended to do right by his family with the press, on social media and at business appearances this month, but for him personally, things were more complicated now. He needed to prepare for the possibility that Isabeau could be carrying his child. She hadn't answered his question about her diabetes and possible complications in pregnancy.

Time here at his house would give him the opportunity to learn more about her, to strategize contingencies. At his house. On his turf.

The charcoal-colored roof peaks of his sanctuary

crested above the tall, impossibly green pine trees. Unlike his mother's sleek home, Trystan's property spoke to the Alaskan wilderness. Maybe not in the same rough-hewn way as the Steele complex. But still, his craftsman ranch house sat amidst trees, overlooking a crisp lake stocked with fish.

His place was part of the family estate, but Trystan had been far more interested in working with the land than the rest of his family. Another mark of his outsider status. He'd invested in horses and property. From the corner of his eye, he caught a glimpse of a buckskin galloping away from the paddock behind the wooden barn that sat off to the back left corner of his house.

Isabeau shifted in her seat next to him, seeming to respond to the bumps in the rough, pebble-littered road. Her eyes darted to the back seat where she'd secured Paige with a seat belt harness. "The photos of your ranch don't do it justice. This is beautiful, especially the way stones in the structure echo the landscape. You have a slice of heaven here."

"Thank you," he said simply, moved by her admiration, more so than he wanted to admit even to himself. "We can take a tour of the stables and land tomorrow, once you've had a chance to settle in."

"I would like that." She pressed a hand to her mouth, stifling a yawn. "Sorry about that. It's been a long day."

"I've heard pregnancy makes women tired."

"So does travel."

"That it does." He draped a hand over the steering wheel. "You never did answer the question about if your diabetes could be of concern if you're expecting. Is that something you've ever discussed with your physician?"

"I've been in a doctor's care since my teenage years, and yes, I asked once, wondering if I would be able to have children at all." She nibbled at her bottom lip. "My imagination had concocted all sorts of scary scenarios. But my doctor allayed my fears. She said an obstetrician would monitor my blood sugar levels and blood pressure more closely. That I would need to be more stringent in my dietary choices. They'd use ultrasounds to check the baby's size, since diabetes can make the infant larger. It's manageable. Does that answer your question?"

"Yes, thank you." A surge of protectiveness swept over him with every item she listed, and he made fast work of parking his car.

He employed a couple in their fifties to oversee housekeeping and the stables. Dedicated and with a sense of humor he enjoyed, they'd helped him growing up, neighbors of his deadbeat parents. And now he was grateful to be able to help them in return. He introduced Isabeau to Gena and Lou knowing they would help her settle in faster than he could.

Isabeau was in safe hands, and quickly on her

way up to her suite—freeing him to move forward with some business of his own.

Leaving Isabeau to rest in one of the guest rooms, he moved toward his own sleeping quarters, needing a moment to collect his thoughts. And to check on the state of his family. Especially his brother. Since the blowup at the wedding, he hadn't heard from Chuck. He and his wife, Shana, had left shortly after things ignited between Trystan and Isabeau. Chuck's marriage had been strained by their trying for a child. Years of infertility had them tense and grieving.

How would they feel if Isabeau was expecting? Would they be able to celebrate or would it bring more pain?

The door to his room opened with a slight creak, revealing a sun-soaked private space.

Home.

No doubt about it. Here, on the outskirts of Juneau, this was his element. Cathedral ceilings characterized by exposed, crisscrossed wooden beams. He took a moment in the door frame, appreciating this life. This simple moment that he wouldn't have again for a while since he'd be serving as the face of the merged businesses.

From here, his eye roved past the massive wooden sleigh bed decorated in burnt orange and mustard yellow. Instead of focusing on the decor, he let the view of the mountain settle him, thankful for the massive windows that provided an uninterrupted view of the wild that whispered to his restless soul.

Striding into the room, he closed the distance to the leather sitting area for the best view of the snow-topped mountain. Stepping over the deer-skin rug, the same deerskin rug he'd made with his father and Chuck many, many years ago, he searched for his silver laptop.

Time to call his brother.

He found his laptop on the rustic antler-and-glass side table by the leather love seat. Leather groaned as he settled into the massive, ergonomic office chair. He turned the computer on and pulled up the video chat application.

When Chuck answered the call in the sprawling library that he also used as an office, he appeared calm, ever in control, the family leader since their father had died. And clearly working in spite of his insistence that he was taking time off. Fatigue set in his jaw, and the normal fire that danced in his eyes seemed stymied.

Knowing his brother wouldn't offer up personal information without being prodded, Trystan cleared his throat. "How's it going? Everything settle out okay?"

Sighing, Chuck ran his hand through his flared blond hair. "Sure, temporary peace restored."

"Temporary?"

"Marriage is…complicated." He shrugged his shoulders, sagging in the ill-lit study.

Trystan could just make out book spine silhouettes lining the shelves in the background Chuck pinched the bridge of his nose, exhaustion stamped on his face.

"I'll take your word for that, Chuck." Sympathy for his brother pushed through his own muddled head over his limbo state with Isabeau. "Is there anything I can do?"

"I appreciate your call. That means more than you can know."

"It's tough to know what to do. I don't want to butt into your private business."

"You're my brother. And hell," he chuckled hoarsely, exhaustion in every tone, "you're saving my ass by stepping in for me as the face of the company. I know this isn't your gig." Picking up a nearby bear paper weight, Chuck shook his head. Guilt seemed to settle in the lines of his face. He stopped examining the paperweight to look at Trystan in the camera. The picture of brotherly sincerity. "I owe you."

Trystan waved his hand, half grinning. "Hey, you can come shovel out the horse stalls sometime."

"Deal."

As he thought about the way talking to his brother had helped him, he wondered if maybe he'd been missing an obvious source of assistance in his pursuit of Isabeau. "Is Alyana still staying with you and Shana?"

"Yes, she is. Do you want me to have her call

you? Or I can just bring her here. She's in the next room."

"Please. That would be great if you could get her. And take care, brother. Call me if you need me."

"Will do," Chuck said before disappearing from the screen.

Trystan questioned the wisdom of this, but he was fast learning from Isabeau that there were arenas of his life where it was prudent to ask for assistance. His younger sister stepped into view, willowy and shy, but sharp, in a way that came as a surprise because it was unexpected from such an unassuming source.

"Hello, Trystan. I see you made it home. I hope all's going well with the consultant. She seemed nice at the wedding."

"She is very effective and…" He hesitated over what was too mild a word to describe Isabeau, but over-the-top words weren't his style and would generate more attention among his siblings than this call and his questions already would. "Yes, she *is* nice. Very nice. And that's why I'm calling. I need your help."

"Before we start, let's be clear." A small laugh accompanied Alayna's raised hand. "I'm not going to take over your appearances."

"That's not why I'm calling."

She crinkled her freckled nose. "You're going to make me feel guilty about not helping, and I hate that."

"Because it works. You're a softie."

"I don't have the luxury of hiding from our hard-headed older siblings." She toyed with her necklace, no doubt one of the crafts from her small business. "And really, you know I would make a mess of things."

"You're welcome here anytime." Except now. He was hoping for time alone with Isabeau, which brought him back to the reason for his call. "I just need suggestions."

"On what?"

"Things that will impress Isabeau Waters."

A flash of interest sparked in her eyes. "Impress professionally or personally?"

He paused for only a second. "The latter."

She dropped the necklace, suddenly becoming more serious. Focusing on him. "You're kidding me."

"Have I ever been a joker?"

"Not really…" She scrunched her forehead, studying him for a second before continuing, "Okay, then. Women are all different, so there's no set gift or date that will appeal to all. My best advice? Listen to her. Really, really listen. You'll find your clues."

He shook his head. "You can't seriously expect me to sift through that and make heads or tails of it."

She shrugged, but didn't cave. "I can't do the hard work for you. Women are impressed by men who listen. Men who make an effort to understand them."

His temples pinched with a new ache, but he supposed her advice made sense. "And, when I understand her, I'll know what to do?"

"When you listen, you'll discover her passions. The things that are special and important to her." Alayna heaved a sigh, and he wondered if she'd given that speech to any other rock-headed men before.

Something about her tone shouted *yes*.

As he watched his sister sign off, Trystan wished women weren't so damn enigmatic. Clues and a million different answers.

Except he also knew, he'd never been so drawn to a woman the way he was with Isabeau. Which meant…

Time to start searching for something as special and unique as the woman herself.

Isabeau was more than a little surprised by Trystan's home.

Sure, she'd seen photos and done her research about how he'd participated in the building of his house—both literally and financially. But there was peace here in this place that no photos or descriptions could capture.

She could understand why he wouldn't want to leave his private mountain retreat for the corporate grind.

Knees curled to her chest, she sat on her bed,

sinking into the depths of the mattress. Outlines and ideas for press opportunities formed a semicircle around her. A pen passed between her fingertips as she examined a document for a satellite radio show. Paige yawned from across the room. She sat stretched on the white carpet in the abbreviated living space between the bed and the oak-framed fireplace. The dog's corresponding chuff drew Isabeau's eye from fine print to the lazy yellow Lab, and then, once she saw her dog was just sleeping, she soaked in the view.

The sun had already slipped behind the tree line, but her room seemed as dazzling as ever. Everything since she'd met Trystan felt like a dream. One she had to wake up from.

Burying herself back in the documents, she shifted files to the wooden chest at the foot of her bed. Then she paused for a moment to examine media outlets from both television and podcast, and considered the events that would put him in the public eye, from a state fair to a private power broker dinner. Chewing her pen cap, she almost didn't hear the door creak open.

Instantly, the pen cap returned to a more normal, natural position on her thigh. Trystan.

Somehow, even though he leaned in the door frame in muted light, her heart pounded heavy and fast. Awareness ricocheted through her system. She remembered all too well the closeness she'd felt with him before.

Closeness she needed to forget and resist.

Waving a paper in her hand, she said, "You have an interview at a Juneau news outlet next week. I've outlined a list of subjects that could come up so we can talk through your answers."

"I'll tell them the truth." His words, articulated as anticipated. The hard line.

Shaking her head, Isabeau flashed a small, corrective smile. "A polished truth that steers clear of reporter traps. You're an intelligent man. I believe you'll enjoy the challenge."

"Was that a compliment?" He moved into the room, approaching her. Dark eyes inquisitive.

"It's the truth, told with polish." Stacking the papers into a neat pile, she wished he wasn't so appealing all the time. It would make staying on track so much easier.

"Touché." He took the papers and scanned them, shuffling through. "If you'll email me the files, I'll go through them and prep first thing in the morning. After that, I thought we could both use some relaxation, some settling-in time. Maybe it'll give you more of those insights for crafting my image."

Too many insights into this compelling man could be trouble for her considering her level of attraction.

What if she found out she liked him even more?

"What did you have in mind?"

A noncommittal shrug relaxed his shoulders as he sank into the leather armchair in the living space adjacent to the bed. "Your choice. Horseback riding? Kayaking? Dinner out, if that's what you prefer?"

How easy it felt to be near him. Even Paige liked him. Isabeau debated her choices for the outing.

"Any chance we can kayak and whale watch in a way that won't scare me to pieces?" Being with him made taking a risk easier.

Maybe that was because he was the biggest risk of all.

Damn. She was in deep with this man.

He studied her with that steady look of his. "That can be arranged."

In the moment, in *this* moment, Isabeau felt her throat swell up a bit, seeming to stop air and words. His gaze lingered, and her skin heated in response. Though, if she were being honest, her own eyes searched him a moment too long, as well.

Silence passed and electricity built, seeming to hum in the air.

He angled closer. "Is everything satisfactory with your suite?"

"It's lovely." She glanced around the room again, toying with a lock of her hair. "There's everything I could want."

"I made sure there were snacks available. If you

or Paige need something different, just let me know and I'll arrange it."

"Thank you." She chewed her bottom lip. "I know what happened between us at the wedding reception wasn't planned and I hope it won't make things awkward. We have to work together. So any outings we take together are all toward that goal."

"Heard and understood." He nodded quickly.

Her eyes narrowed. "No secret agenda?"

"I am dedicated to doing my best for my family."

"That doesn't sound like an answer."

"I realize things are tense. Let's just say that I intend to do my job, and at the same time we should get to know each other better. Just in case."

Those last three words echoed in her skull. A reminder of why she needed to be professional and focus. If she was pregnant, she would need a successful business life more than ever.

All she could do was nod before he stood up from the chair, a ripple of muscles beneath his cotton shirt. "I'll see you in the morning."

Afternoon sun high in the sky, Trystan sprawled in his kayak, his face tipped to the rays. Summer days stretched long here, and he soaked up as many hours as possible.

The waters off the coast near Juneau weren't as cold as other parts of the state, and he hadn't slept much last night. This was a simple outing to share with Isabeau, one he hoped she would find as soul soothing as he did. A low-key way to ease closer to her, learn more about what made her tick.

Because truth be told, every day with her made him ache all the more to have her in his bed. He had to wonder now why they couldn't use this window of time where they didn't know about a pregnancy to simply explore the attraction, see where it led them.

He could sense she wasn't ready to hear that suggestion yet, but he was a patient man. He had her here, now, out on the water on this awesome summer day, a picnic basket full of food waiting for them in his Range Rover parked on the shore.

But that feast waiting for them held nothing to Isabeau's perfectly curved figure accentuated by the formfitting wet suit, visible even with a life jacket. Despite the warmer waters right now, the wet suit was often a standard part of the kayaking experience in Alaska.

Surveying her for a moment, he watched the way her nose scrunched as she paddled forward, gliding through the water. He had to give the dog credit too. She seemed to take everything in stride, unconcerned by the life jacket and the lack of land in her immediate vicinity. Not even flinching when a pair of wolves had sprinted along the tree line before disappearing into the forest.

He paddled closer, one smooth stroke at a time,

steering into the current. "You know everything about me and I know so little about you." Other than just where to kiss her on her neck to make her sigh with pleasure.

"You didn't run a background check on me like most of my clients?" She paddled as well, her strokes not as efficient as his, but not bad for an amateur.

With practice, she could fit right into this way of life.

He winked. "I figured if the family hired you, you must be right for the job."

"That's quite trusting of you."

"I have my strengths. They have theirs. But I suspect you're dodging my question." He eased his kayak closer to her, bumping the side to adjust the angle so she didn't drift too far from shore.

"There's no massive secret. I grew up in Washington, the Seattle area. My parents…divorced… when I was in elementary school. My mother worked hard to give me the best life possible." She kept her eyes averted, her strokes growing more even the longer they were out on the water.

"Your mother loved you." He could hear it in her voice.

"Yes, she did." She blinked fast, her smile wobbling.

"And your father?"

Her smile thinned. "He decided working less meant he could pay less child support," she said drily. "He went with that plan until he could figure out a way to leave without a trail."

"That's wrong on so many levels." He couldn't imagine a world where he would walk out on his child. Even the thought of being a father had his mind spinning with the ways he would be there for Isabeau and their kid.

If they had one.

His gaze gravitated to her stomach, hidden by a life jacket. A stomach he'd stroked even when their impulsive connection hadn't left much time for ditching clothes and seeing each other. That part, he regretted and hoped to rectify someday soon. The sooner the better.

She paddled in long, even strokes, the sun glinting off her red hair gathered in a topknot. "My mother and I were better off without him, but it still makes me sad she had to work so hard for so long. She remarried to a great guy who treats her well."

"And she still lives in Washington?"

"She did...until she passed away a year ago—lung disease."

"I am so very sorry." Squeezing her hand, he reminded himself of his sister's advice about asking and listening. Learn as much as he could about this fascinating woman—not a hardship at all. "What brought you to Alaska?"

"I wanted a fresh start. Turns out there are plenty of rugged, rich Alaskans in search of an image consultant." She swept her paddle through the water. "Have you ever wanted to live somewhere else?"

He scanned the bay, drinking in the banks filled with lush green grass, the shadow of a bird rippling on the water. Mountains far in the distance. Everything he needed right here. "Nope."

"I thought this time on the water was about getting to know each other better."

"Sorry." He tipped his head back to watch the progress of the eagle soaring through the sky. "Longer answer? I love my home state. I love the land and feel strongly about protecting what we have."

A smile shone in her eyes. "That passion in your voice is exactly what you should bring to interviews." She nodded in affirmation, her topknot listing to the side. "I hear you and Delaney Steele both played a large part in persuading Royce Miller to bring his innovations to Alaska Oil Barons, Inc."

"He just needed to know there were people in the family who genuinely cared about preservation and not just the cost-cutting measures in his pipeline upgrades."

"That's what makes your two families strong, you know. None of you speak as one voice. You each have your own viewpoints and perspectives. No cookie-cutter types."

"I definitely will take that as a compliment."

"Why do you seem so surprised?"

"I think of an image consultant as ironing out all the wrinkles in a personality."

"Not at all. Personality is what captures attention, and that is the ultimate goal. You just want the right kind of attention."

Conversation ceased as a whale crested the water in the distance. Even from here, the kayaks bobbed with the ripples from the massive creature. The beauty of whale watching never ceased to leave him in awe.

But it was nothing in comparison to the beauty of Isabeau's face right now.

"How's your bucket list going today?"

A wide grin—a real one this time—danced across her face. "This is perfect. Thank you."

Her eyes sparkled. Her joy made his breath catch slightly. All he wanted to do was reach over to her kayak and kiss her. Slowly. Deeply. To linger in a way they hadn't during their hasty coupling in the boathouse.

But perhaps a better chance to linger with her would be during the picnic.

Those thoughts were cut short as Paige barked once, twice, full out, calling to him as she pawed at Isabeau. Her eyes glazed over and she swayed. Her paddle fell from her hands, hitting the side of the kayak and then the water. Her lashes fluttered closed as dread filled his gut.

Trystan paddled faster, closing the gap between them but all too aware of how far it was to shore.

Six

Isabeau had learned to live with diabetes as a teen. But her body's lack of cooperation still frustrated her. Swaying, she forced her eyes open again. She gripped the sides of the kayak to keep herself from flipping as she sought to right the world wobbling in front of her woozy gaze.

Dimly, she registered Paige barking an alert— usually she pawed, then whimpered. A bark meant Paige was moving on to the big guns since Isabeau hadn't heeded the first levels of warning. She tried to focus, to form words.

Words eluded her, but she saw Trystan paddling

toward her with concern on his face. Help was on the way. She wasn't alone. She simply had to hold on.

What an alien feeling to have someone to lean on so she could experience life more fully without worrying about what-ifs with her health. She could boat and watch the whales. And while she was sad the outing was done, how awesome to have experienced it.

With Trystan.

Paige's barking decreased to a whimper as Trystan drew closer, stroke by stroke. Her dog seemed to recognize his help.

"Talk to me, Isabeau," Trystan's voice carried over the rippling water. "What can I do to help you?"

His words cleared away more of the fog.

"I'm okay. Just light-headed." Her hand shaking, she reached into the waterproof box hooked to her kayak. "I'm eating a snack now. I'll be fine." She found a packet of almonds and popped a handful into her mouth, chewing slowly.

He grunted. Trystan looped a rope through the hook on the front of her kayak and paddled out front. With powerful strokes, he headed for shore, pulling her boat after his. She kept popping almonds in her mouth, feeling her vision steady with each bite. She should feel guilty about him having to haul her back to shore, but he paddled so effortlessly, he didn't seem at all fazed. Muscles rippled along his arms in the wet suit.

Her mouth watered.

She was definitely feeling better. "I'm sorry to have scared you," she called out to him. "And I'm really sorry to have ruined our outing."

"I shouldn't have pushed you to overdo it." His words came out tight with self-recrimination.

"I'm an adult. I know my limits and I came prepared." She finished off the last almond and continued, "Everything's fine. Paige did her job."

He grunted again. With a final sweep of the paddle, his kayak slid up onto the shore. He stepped out into the shallows, water lapping against his knees and hauled her kayak the rest of the way. He extended a hand and took her arm, bracing her as she swung her legs over the wide body of the boat and found her footing. They made their way to the rocky shoreline, Paige splashing alongside.

He eased her to a sitting position and beached the kayaks while her dog shook the water off and settled by her feet.

Trystan returned to kneel by her. "We should go home."

"I'm okay now." She tried to stand but he kept a hand on her shoulder. "Truly, Trystan. I let myself get caught up in the moment and didn't listen to Paige fast enough. Thank goodness she was insistent. Let me just check my A1C level to be sure."

She tunneled her hand into the waterproof bag and pulled out a small pouch and her cell phone.

She noticed him wincing when she pricked the side of her finger and tested the blood. Funny how she didn't even think about it, she was so used to living with the condition.

Reading the results, she smiled in relief. "All's good. I'll just log it into the app on my phone, then recheck later. Thank you for your help and for being concerned."

"Of course. I just wish I'd paid closer attention and noticed signs sooner—"

"You couldn't have known." She braced a hand on his chest, the hard wall of muscle warm beneath her palm.

Her fingers twitched with the urge to explore. His pupils widened with awareness as his eyes narrowed, lasering in on her.

Her throat moved in a long swallow, and she couldn't resist the need to lick her lips. His gaze flickered over her mouth, lingering.

"Isabeau," he said simply, his voice husky.

She knew she should push him away. She'd promised herself she would keep him at arm's length. And yet she ached for him, ached for his kiss, ached to find out if she'd imagined their explosive connection.

Before she could finish the thought, she swayed toward him. Her eyes slid closed as their lips met and she melted into the sensation. The salty scent of him. The strength of his arms around her. The echo of the husky growl in his throat.

Her fingers crawled up his chest to his cheek, bristly from an afternoon shadow. Everything about the kiss was more than she remembered. Maybe because they were in the bright sunlight that left a glow even behind her closed eyes. The wind rolling in off the water gave an expansive feeling to the moment, uncontained by walls. The taste of him was crisp and tangy, and it stirred a hunger that seared her veins with every throbbing heartbeat.

And as she angled away from a kiss that had to end because taking it further was too dangerous, she couldn't escape the truth.

She'd just made a huge mistake.

Because now she wanted him more than ever.

He couldn't decide if kissing Isabeau had been a good idea or not. She'd clearly wanted him, and he'd been off balance from the scare of her nearly passing out in the kayak, and he vowed to do some internet research on diabetes once he was home.

And he also vowed that one impulsive kiss would not derail his bigger goal of winning her into his bed.

After she'd pulled back, she'd been all business again, talking about them packing the boats and eating their picnic food in the car instead as they returned to the house. She had emails to check and calls to return. And he'd lost track of all she'd listed. He'd been more focused on watching her, gauging her mood and deciding how best to proceed.

For now, he'd decided that since she wanted to ignore the kiss, he would go along with that. It was certainly better than having her declare it couldn't happen again.

Progress of sorts.

A progress that gave an extra kick to his steps as he walked into his great room after showering.

To find Isabeau waiting.

For the moment at least, she seemed unaware of his presence, which gave him an opportunity to study her.

Her hair was piled on her head, glistening with dampness. So she had showered too. She'd changed into leggings and a flowing white shirt that called to his hands to tunnel underneath.

But he was learning that slow and steady was the better move with her. He didn't want her to run, the way she had after their encounter at the boathouse. He needed to use their time together wisely.

Striding deeper into the room, he looked closer and what he found surprised him. He'd expected to discover her with her computer or tablet, but instead she was…pulling yarn out of a bag. Shock left him too surprised to ask why she wasn't answering all those emails and calls she'd mentioned back at the water.

Legs tucked to her side, Isabeau fished a crochet hook from her blue paisley bag, settling deeper into the left side of the light tan sofa.

She looked up at him, her red hair falling into her face slightly, contrasting with those bright blue eyes. "What's with the frown?"

"I'm just…surprised, maybe even a little confused."

"I'm just crocheting." She tugged more of the yarn free.

A few strides took him past Isabeau and the living area to the outer wall made entirely of windows. From over his shoulder, he called, "Why?"

"It's relaxing and productive at the same time. I decided to give myself a chance to settle before getting back to work." She shifted her legs to the other side, tucking a throw pillow behind her.

Scanning the horizon, he took a steadying breath. Concern for her health—and maybe an unborn baby's health—weighed heavily on his mind, despite the normally calming effects of the sprawling landscape peppered with pines and other evergreens.

Since the construction of this ranch-inspired building, Trystan had felt, even if it wasn't a permanent feeling, at home here. If there were ever a physical building that fit his state of mind, it was this place. Every detail reflected Trystan's soul, from the carved wooden figurines of moose and bears to the sweeping panorama of the Alaskan wilderness supplied by the wall of windows.

After a few moments, he made his way back to the hearth and sofa area where Isabeau sat with her yarn. "How do you feel?"

"I feel great. Really." She smiled reassuringly. "And yes, I checked my blood sugar levels to be on the safe side, and all is well. It was just one of those things. They happen, not often, but that's my life. I'm sorry you were worried."

He sat beside her and tapped the tan-colored yarn. "What are you making?"

"Scarves for local homeless shelters."

Not what he'd expected to hear. "That's really kind of you."

"What goes around comes around," she mumbled so softly he almost didn't hear her.

"It would be good if more people thought that way." He and his family had so much that sometimes, no matter how many charity foundations they set up, he wondered what more they could be doing. He felt a twinge of conscience about not giving enough of his attention to the upcoming wilderness initiative fund-raiser. Isabeau was here to help him and still he found her a major, tantalizing distraction. "When did you start crocheting scarves for homeless shelters?"

"And blankets and hats. My mother and I were

gifted with some of each when I was a young teen-ager."

Shock knocked him off balance for a beat. He blinked through it and willed his face to stay neutral. "You were homeless?"

"After my dad ran off for a while and we got evicted. We were only in a shelter for a couple of weeks, but it saved us." Her fingers worked deftly, yarn transformed from static string to the beginnings of a scarf.

She didn't look at him.

She didn't move, other than her fingers.

"I'm so sorry." He understood what it was like to have your world uprooted by turmoil, but he'd always known he had a place to live.

"No need to be sorry. I'm here and successful and okay. There was this little old lady there who crocheted for us."

"As a volunteer or staff member?" he asked, enjoying the sound of her voice and appreciating her opening up to him.

"A former resident. She understood what it was like and that was her way of giving back." Isabeau's eyes took on a pensive air, as if seeing inward to the past, looping yarn over the crochet hook faster and faster. "She helped me while Mom searched for a job. It was summer, so school was out. We sat and she showed me how to crochet."

He searched for something to say, but words

weren't his strength, and it wasn't like he could ask her to coach him on this. "You're really talented."

She glanced at him quickly, half smiling. "Just because someone's poor doesn't mean they have to be grateful for donations that look like crap."

"Good point."

She laughed softly. "You still seem confused though."

Such an understatement. When his family had approached him about working with an image consultant, he figured he'd be working with a vapid woman only interested in the veneer of things. Not one whose heart had such depth. Now, after meeting Isabeau, he felt a splash of embarrassment for his initial assessment of an image consultant stereotype. "I just didn't expect an image consultant to be so…deep."

"I'll try not to be insulted." She yanked free a length of yarn before setting to work again.

"I've made no secret of the fact I'm participating in this makeover under duress. I'm just not that into superficial appearances."

"People gain confidence in different ways, and if that confidence is used to do good for others, then this—" she held up the scarf in progress "—helps me more than the receiver."

Those bright eyes met his and she lifted her project to show him the small progress. He could almost see a younger Isabeau—the one in the shelter, gain-ing confidence because an old woman had given her a fine scarf.

"Yes. You're definitely a surprise." Leaning toward her, he studied her face, the way her fingers moved, the careful attention to the smallest detail.

He studied her mouth.

"Well, thank goodness I'm not boring." She took her bottom lip between her teeth, releasing it slowly.

A bolt of desire shot straight through him. Electrifying him. "Lady, you are far from boring."

More than air, he wanted to kiss her again. Holding back was difficult as hell. But something told him this wasn't the time to press her on that—or more. He didn't want to spook her and lose ground.

He was definitely making progress. So the best bet?

Double down with another outing to romance her.

Later that week, Isabeau wondered when she'd lost control of her client.

When he'd kissed her? Or when he'd looked at her with a passion so intense it seared her?

After she'd steadied her blood sugar and nerves with some good old-fashioned crocheting, she'd spent the evening locking down a schedule of podcast interviews for Trystan.

Only to have him surprise her with the announcement of another planned outing. As she'd started to argue that work needed to come first, he'd surprised her yet again by revealing he'd set up a publicity opportunity on his own. He'd secured a news interview at a gold rush festival in Juneau.

She tightened her hold on Paige's leash as they walked through the festival goers, proud of her dog's firm focus in such a melee. Boy, was there a lot to take in. Surveying the crowd, she had to admit that although this might not have been an event she'd have set up for Trystan, the festival was full of life.

Chain saws hummed in the distance from the woodcutting competition where woodsmen—and women—showed off their prowess carving art from huge logs of Alaskan pine. The scent of fresh sawdust, sweet and sap-tinged, hung in the air everywhere they explored. A small livestock show nearby kept kids entertained with a petting zoo where eager goats cavorted for the reward of a treat. And now, she paused as she heard the cheers of another crowd near the band pavilion.

For a moment, she lingered, watching a lean twentysomething brunette hoist an axe above her head and aim at a target fifty paces away with surprising accuracy. A small crowd made up of older couples and young families cheered, loosing whistles and whoops of approval into the air. Beaming, the young woman took a mock bow before nodding to the next competitor.

Guitars and a banjo played in the background

providing a peppy beat for their wanderings. Navigating through throngs of people gathered outside food trucks and the lines for inflatable slides, Isabeau felt strangely at peace.

Rather than continuing to watch another competition—this time with two men racing against each other to climb a pole—she slid her attention to Trystan, who walked confidently beside her. His muddied cognac-brown cowboy boots were paired with worn jeans and a red flannel shirt, sleeves straining against his muscled arms.

Damn. Sexy as ever.

Isabeau cleared her throat, elbowing him. "This was a fantastic idea. I'm impressed."

"Pleased to hear it. This is one of my favorite festivals. And it seemed a good platform to talk about ways we Alaskans are working to responsibly cultivate our resources."

"And I'm impressed again. You have more of a way with words than you give yourself credit for." Or than she'd given him credit for. When he was in his comfort zone, he was spot-on. "I can see you being one of those old-school gold miners, forging your way through the Alaskan frontier, living in a tent."

She couldn't quite make out his eyes from the shade cast by the brim of his simple Stetson.

He laughed softly. "Sounds like heaven to me. In fact, I wouldn't even need the tent. Just give me a hammock to string between two trees and a thermal sleeping bag."

A line of elementary school–age children walked by, laughing as they clutched cotton candy puffs that wavered in the wind in time with the banjo music. Such a sense of community.

"You fit in well here," she said, noting how many people who recognized him waved and smiled. He was so…accessible. Not as distant as he'd seemed in more formal settings. Guilt pinched her. No matter how much she told herself she was tailoring his makeover to fit his personality, she saw the truth. He was a happy and whole person right here, right now, no changes. "This month will be over soon and you can go back to living at your ranch full-time, sleeping bag and all." Although she couldn't help but think how Naomi had mentioned the possibility of him taking a more active role beyond this month. Would the business still want her services long term?

More importantly, would she still be spending close quarters time with Trystan long term?

"I'll miss you." He nudged back his Stetson, and his deep blue eyes met hers, locking her in place.

Her skin tingled, and the noisy, packed world faded away for an instant. "We've only been working together a little over a week."

"Then that should tell you what an impression you've made on me in such a short time."

"I have a job to do." And this flirting made it tougher. How would she resist him if their lives were tied together permanently through a child?

"And I'm asking you to consider the possibility we could see more of each other. You work on a consultant basis. You could take time off. Money's not an issue. These are the sorts of things to consider, especially if there's a baby."

There it was. The issue that clouded everything else.

This special outing, his flirting—none of it was just about dating each other. They'd made that kind of casual relationship impossible by impulsively sleeping together. As much as she'd vowed not to live her mother's life, vulnerable and alone for so many years, Isabeau had not made the wisest choices lately.

"I won't be dependent on anyone, particularly a man I'm sleeping with."

He fell silent, clearly digesting her assertion.

But before Trystan could lobby a response, Isabeau saw a news crew out of the corner of her eye.

Saved by the media.

Not a phrase she used every day. Relief washed over her. "News crew at your two o'clock." Isabeau nodded in the direction of the huddle of journalists gathered outside a funnel cake stand.

The female reporter—high heels sinking in a mud puddle—tapped her cameraman on the shoulder. A mutual recognition, Isabeau realized. The cameraman adjusted the gear on his shoulder, and the news media team began their approach.

"Time for my debut," Trystan muttered, motioning for Isabeau to follow.

"Mr. Mikkelson," the reporter called, waving. "I'm so glad you and your girlfriend could meet with us for an exclusive."

Isabeau blinked in shock.

Girlfriend?

Seven

A half hour later, as they settled into the SUV, Isabeau was still steaming over being maneuvered.

She'd been so immersed in the beautiful day with Trystan that she'd never seen it coming.

Now, he guided the rental vehicle from the packed parking lot, and she watched the fairgrounds grow smaller in the rearview mirror as her regrets grew larger.

She'd been drawn to Trystan, succumbing to that chemistry, because she'd thought he was giving her the personal space she'd requested while they waited for pregnancy results.

Instead, he was just setting her up for his own

agenda. To press and push for…what? Either to get her to sleep with him again or ensure some kind of hold over her if it turned out she carried his child.

She glanced down at her stomach, then over at him, his hands so sure on the steering wheel.

As if he felt her gaze, he looked back at her. "I didn't tell her that."

Sure, whatever.

"The damage is done. The story's going to run and it will say that I have a personal relationship with a client." She hugged herself, agitation rising. "Denying the report won't do any good."

"Then let's do the opposite and play it up as a great romance. People do fall for each other on the job. Letting the public know we're dating could prep for news if you're pregnant—"

"I know, I know. There will be no hiding the truth. But what if I'm not and we've convinced the world we're having some great love story?"

"We'll quietly break up…if that's what you wish."

His hesitation gave her pause as well, and launched a surprise flurry of butterflies in her stomach. "If that's what *I* want? Are you saying— after a little over a week together—that you're madly in love with me?"

"Of course not. But I've made no secret of the fact I would like to see more of you." He reached across the space to stroke her shoulder. "Come on, let's enjoy the rest of the day. We could even turn around and go back, take in another part of the festival, get something to eat."

"How can you just drop a bombshell like that and then say let's have a funnel cake?"

"There's nothing we can do about the past except enjoy the future." He nudged his Stetson up, sliding his sunglasses in place.

Easier said than done.

"It's been a full day. If you don't mind, I would like to get a quiet meal and turn in early. Or maybe you've already planned for us to go to the airport?"

"Actually, no. I filed the flight plan for the morning."

Her back went straight with suspicion. This was too much. Paige nudged Isabeau's foot from the floorboard of the front seat. "Trystan—"

He raised a hand in defense. "I had to plan it for tomorrow because of weather tonight, which I only learned about when we landed. I was going to tell you at the festival. I have arranged for a hotel suite for us so we don't have to drive the couple of hours back and forth to the ranch—and yes, the suite has two bedrooms. I've also had some clothes sent over for both of us, along with arranging for Paige's needs, as well."

Guilt nudged a lot harder than her dog. She melted back into the seat. "I'm sorry if I sound like an ingrate. You're being very thoughtful."

"I am not setting you up." He shot her a pointed look. "But make no mistake, I am working my ass off to impress you."

She bit her lip hard to keep from telling him the truth—it was working.

Trystan had learned a lesson at the Juneau festival.

He needed Isabeau—in more ways than one.

She brought a light and sparkle to his world when he saw it through her eyes. His practical, blunt nature tended to miss the beauty in a moment and, yes, the nuances, as well.

He'd been certain he'd set up the perfect day for her, down to an interview that would show her his work ethic. Instead, the reporter had surprised the hell out of him. Not to mention setting back his progress with Isabeau. If he'd included her in the plans, she surely would have arranged that interview to their benefit and had the reporter eating out of the palm of her hand.

Instead, he'd walked them into a media trap.

Tonight, in the five-star, waterside hotel suite, he would have to tread warily. At least she was relaxing in the small, saltwater pool on the screened-in balcony. The waters were warmed. He'd seen her head out in a swimsuit, sexy as hell, even though he would have preferred they enjoy the bubbling waters together, naked.

But he sure wasn't walking away from this chance to be with her, to get closer.

He'd ordered a light, tapas-style dinner to eat while lounging in recliners in the shallow end—Alaskan crab tacos, fresh tortilla chips and a fruit salsa, trying to keep her health issues in mind. Stepping out on the enclosed balcony, he heard acoustic classics piped in softly through the sound system.

Isabeau glanced over her shoulder, the creamy flesh drawing him closer. "Trystan, hello. Thank you for this restful evening. This is lovely." She gestured toward the shoreline and mountain view. "No matter how long I'm here, I just can't get over the beauty of Alaska."

"I'm glad you're pleased." And he owed his sister a huge thanks for her suggestions.

She lifted a taco from the silver platter by the pool, held it over a napkin and took a bite, savoring it. "And this is definitely better than a funnel cake."

Kneeling beside her, he thumbed the corner of her mouth. "This is most definitely a better way to spend the day with you."

"I'm wearing a swimsuit." She raised an eyebrow and took another bite of the taco.

Yes, he knew, but he didn't see the need to point out he'd been waiting for her. "I fully expected you would. I'm wearing swim trunks, as well."

"Thank you. Maybe it seems silly given we've…" She trailed off, nibbling at the last of her food.

"Not silly at all." He pulled off the hotel robe and sat on the edge of the other lounger in the shallow end. They were here together. He was making progress with her again.

"It's only that I think we need to keep things simple until we know where we stand in a few weeks." She ate the last bite of her crab taco and set aside the napkin on the tiny table.

"Understood." The thought that she might be carrying his child sent a protective surge through him again. Each time he considered their future, the feeling grew stronger.

"Your eyes don't say you're backing off." She reached for her sparkling water with lemon.

"I hope my eyes say that I hear you." He forced himself to relax, resting his elbows on his knees. "My mother—Jeannie—taught me to be respectful to women, so I won't push anything you don't want. But my father also taught me to pursue what I want."

"I would love to hear more about him. I only know what's in the business reports about Charles Mikkelson."

Trystan saw wariness in her eyes, so he settled on sharing a bit of his past to put her at ease. "My father—my adopted dad—loved competing in the Iditarod Trail Sled Dog Race. Every year, our family gathered to cheer him on. Even when I was only their cousin, they would invite me."

Apparently his words were working to soothe her because she turned to face him, dipping her toes into the water. "Have you ever joined the race?"

"I tagged along with him the year before he died. I wish I hadn't waited so long." He averted his eyes, looking out at the harbor full of boats, the sun still shining in a long Alaskan summer day.

"I can tell how much you miss him."

He glanced back at her. "I do. He shouldn't have died so young. He was healthy, active, got his checkups. But he was a workaholic and the stress killed him." He missed Charles Mikkelson every day, the man who'd been the only real father he'd ever known.

"How can you be sure it was stress?"

"I know it in my gut. That makes it tough for me to root for this merger. It's going to put my whole family in the middle of power plays at an even higher level."

"Perhaps the collective effort of working together will distribute the work." She angled toward him, her feet brushing against his.

"Doubtful, but something to hope for." He stroked the arch of her foot with his toe.

Her eyes narrowed, but she didn't pull away. "Tell me more about the race and the family gatherings."

"The Iditarod is named for the trail, and the race

can take anywhere from eight to eleven days depending on the weather conditions."

"I've lived here for two years and I find it inconceivable to think of eleven days in the elements." She stroked her fingers through the frothing waters.

"That's our Alaska." His gaze gravitated to the mountain view. His home. "The trail was used by Inuits hundreds of years before the Russian fur traders came in around the 1800s. Coal miners and other traders used it too. The race is an important part of our culture, even more so now that snowmobiles have all but made dog sledding extinct."

"What about the dogs? Isn't it…um…" She looked at Paige sleeping on the floor by the pool, then back at him, her blue eyes concerned.

"There are groups that feel the race is cruel to the dogs, but the commission responded to those criticisms with stricter monitoring and punishments for those who don't care properly for their dogs. There's debate, and I can't speak to everyone. But I know my father's dogs were a part of our family life. Dad would lose a race before harming his dogs. If a pup didn't show joy for the run, then that pup wasn't a sled dog." He nodded toward Paige. "The same way she was screened for the right job for her."

Isabeau nodded slowly, pensively. "I've heard it said that the moment a dog opens its eyes, he or she is searching for a purpose, a job, whether that be as a house pet or service dog."

"Or search and rescue or agility… Yes, that's the way I see it. I have a purpose too, and it's not to head a company. I'm made to run the ranch, to commune with the land." But he was also honor bound to protect his siblings and their stake in their father's legacy.

It's what Charles would have wanted him to do.

"The turmoil of this merger, the way they need you to help—it won't last forever."

"I know that."

"But you also can't exclude yourself from all family events just because you don't like crowds or the spotlight. You're lucky to have so many people who love you and care about you."

"What about you?" He settled back onto the lounger, some of the deep tension seeping from him—tension that had started with this business merger. "Are you living your dream? What if you couldn't live in a city, building celebrities?"

She set aside her glass of sparkling water, shifting uncomfortably. He seemed to have a touched a nerve, but had no idea how.

She started to stand, the V of her emerald swimsuit offering a tantalizing view of her breasts. "I may have reached my limit in the pool."

He touched her arm lightly, concerned by the skittishness in her eyes. While he wanted her, he absolutely needed her to feel the same. "You're safe with me. I mean it. Nothing happens unless you're on board too."

After a second's hesitation, she settled back into the tub. "That's important to know… Paige doesn't just alert to diabetes. She also alerts to my anxiety and helps me during an attack."

He didn't want to assume and guess wrong. "Could you explain what you mean?"

"In addition to diabetes, I have generalized anxiety disorder." She met his gaze defensively. "In certain situations, I have panic attacks. She has quite a few tasks she can perform, but a couple of examples… Paige uses pressure therapy to alert and soothe me. If I come home and am afraid someone could be lurking inside, she can clear the house, checking every room."

She rushed on, that defensive brace to her shoulders only strengthening. "Some people confuse service dogs and emotional support animals. An emotional support animal is an untrained pet that provides comfort. He or she can't be denied access to rental property if there's a doctor's note, but the pet can't go into restaurants and such. A service dog is a highly trained animal, performing specific tasks and granted public access but expected to behave. I know I'm babbling, but so many people just don't know the difference. And there's still a lot of education needed regarding service dogs for PTSD and anxiety."

"It's okay, Isabeau. You don't need to explain or justify to me. You're impressive and so is Paige." As much as he'd wanted to learn more about her tonight, he hated hearing that she grappled with worries that might get in the way of her happiness. Many pieces of things she'd said before came together in his mind, finally making sense. "You mentioned that you prefer to be behind the camera."

"That's a part of it, yes."

"I'm very sorry," he said and meant it. He wished he'd known earlier so he could have moved forward more carefully. Not that it stopped him from wanting her.

"Take the pity out of your eyes. I have health issues, but I'm not made of eggshells and I'm taking care of myself. This is my life. I'm a survivor and I'm pleased with the life I've built. Paige enables me to experience that life to the fullest."

He stayed quiet, knowing better than to push her further, but her revelation certainly roused more questions for him.

"You're curious about the cause of my panic attacks."

"That's your business to share if you wish."

"Thank you. I appreciate your sensitivity on the subject—and the fact you don't have a horrified expression on your face means a lot to me."

"I'm glad I passed your test." He found himself

looking toward Paige, grateful to know the full extent of the dog's purpose.

She laughed slightly. "I didn't think of it as a test, but I guess maybe it was, subconsciously."

She turned to face him and continued, "The anxiety attacks started young, with those times we were homeless. There were some hairy situations in shelters and even with some of my mom's boyfriends. And then—" she swallowed hard before pressing ahead "—I had a boyfriend in college who didn't like it when I told him we were through. He stalked me afterward, even after restraining orders and jail time."

Paige whimpered, then inched over to rest her head on the side of the spa tub in a sign of comfort Trystan now fully recognized. The realization of what she'd gone through sucker punched him.

Ah hell. He wished he'd known Isabeau then, that he could have somehow been there to protect her. "That's the reason you moved to Alaska."

"Yes. Even though I feel safer here, the jumpiness and the fears that spiral into anxiety still linger." She draped a hand over the side of the spa tub and stroked her dog's head. "Paige senses when those panic attacks are coming on. She does things like pressure therapy against my leg to alert and relax me. In a situation where I'm feeling crowded, smothered even, by crowds, I may give her the 'space' command. She'll walk a circle around me, which keeps people back. In a restaurant, I'll tell her to 'watch my six.' She faces the other way, watching behind me and lets me know if anyone is approaching me."

"That's really amazing." The connection between her and her dog had never appeared stronger to him than right now.

"She is my lifeline in so many ways."

"I never would have guessed she was doing double duty."

"That's the whole idea, that she inconspicuously does her job and hopefully catches an issue before it becomes a major incident. If possible."

He couldn't miss the trust it took for her to reveal the deeper truth behind her dog. "I appreciate your sharing this with me."

"You keep talking about wanting a relationship of some sort." She paused, staring down at her fingers as they combed through the shallow water. "And I need for you to understand things are very complicated with me."

He stayed right where he was, but locked his gaze with hers. "I hear you. And I'm not deterred."

Somehow that look felt as intimate as any kiss. Something had changed between them, something he hadn't anticipated and wasn't completely sure he understood—

His cell phone chimed from across the room and Isabeau startled.

He shook his head, damning the device. "Ignore it."

"You should—"

The ringing stopped.

"See," he said, "no chime for a message. Must not have been important."

The ringing started again.

"Really, Trystan," she said, rising from the pool lounger, the sight of her curves in a sleek emerald one-piece ramping up his pulse. "You should get it."

She tugged on the fluffy robe and he surrendered.

For now.

He hefted himself from the water, grabbing a towel on the way to his phone. He snatched his cell from the patio table and saw his brother Chuck's number.

"Yeah," Trystan barked. "What's going on?"

"Sorry to call so late, but there's been an accident at one of our pipeline construction sites."

"Damn." Trystan said under his breath, tucking the phone between his chin and shoulder as he wrapped the towel around his waist. "Was anyone hurt?"

"Minor injuries, all being treated," Chuck assured him, but his voice was heavy with foreboding. "Protestors are already flocking to the area, along with the press. We need this assessed and handled. I know this isn't what you signed on for when you stepped up to help this month. If you need me—"

"No, I've got it. You're where you need to be."

"Thanks, brother. I don't want the Steeles thinking we can't hold up our end of things and elbowing us out."

"Understood. I'm on my way." On his way into what could be a media hell storm. "Fill me in on the details."

As he listened, he gestured to Isabeau and wrote on a notepad for her to read.

Get ready to leave. Accident with the pipeline. Media/Protesters gathering. Will need your help.

Trystan needed her help.

Those simple written words had seared themselves into Isabeau's brain as she packed and then, once the weather had cleared in the morning, flew with him to the pipeline accident, the plane landing on a nearby stretch of water. Maybe she was feeling vulnerable after all they'd shared in the Jacuzzi.

But she couldn't deny the swell of pride that he'd acknowledged what she had to offer.

She'd never been to a pipeline construction site before, and it surprised her to see just how remote the facility was. So remote they'd jumped in the small plane to get here and Trystan had landed on a stretch of bare earth alongside the work site. Unlike the journey to Trystan's ranch, the flight toward damage control had been a blur of snow-capped mountains and evergreen trees. During the flight, she'd gone over some media ground rules for this scenario. While this particular event was out of her wheelhouse, Isabeau knew how to craft and spin a narrative. They would frame the story and put out all associated media fires.

He was a couple of yards away, gesturing toward the ring of trucks around the site while the foreman made notes. It was difficult to hear over the protestors shouting and blasting music, just past the trucks. They congregated near their bus and a couple of tents to protect them from the elements. Clearly, they were geared up to stick around.

Thankfully, no oil had actually spilled. Isabeau sent up a small prayer of thanks for that. Still, the gathering news media lingered outside the chain-link fence. Their cameras looked unnatural against the skinny pine trees reaching skyward.

Protestors armed with signs gathered, starting rhythmic chants. "Hey, hey. Oh, oh. These pipelines have got to go. Hey, hey. Oh, oh…"

Surveying the crowd, she guessed there were about seventy-five protestors and half a dozen news crews. Not too bad, but serious enough to warrant alarm.

Trystan had jumped right in, speaking, navigating the concerns of both conservation activist Delaney Steele and the pipeline construction workers. Though he'd vowed this wasn't his element, Isabeau couldn't help but notice how smoothly he directed comments and offered strategies. In some ways, the chaos here echoed and complemented the chaos of a ranch. Perhaps that was why he'd been asked to step up. Same skill set, different beast.

The ever-eccentric and brilliant Royce Miller appeared from behind Isabeau, flanked by his fiancée, Naomi, the official lawyer of the Alaska Oil Barons empire. Even from her spot on the sidelines, Isabeau registered the determination in Naomi's eyes as she assessed the situation, her hands resting on her pregnant stomach.

Royce's work boots crunching on gravel as he joined Trystan and the foreman. As the research engineer brought on for ensuring safer pipelines, Royce's presence here was critical. After all, as she understood things, it was his innovative design that had kept the oil from spilling over in this accident. That piece of information would come in handy when fielding media questions. The company had ceased activity on the pipeline as soon as the malfunction occurred. Another snippet of data that would help defuse this situation.

Naomi stopped alongside Isabeau, hugging her long sweater around her as the wind whipped through the work site. "How's it going with prepping Trystan?"

Isabeau angled her head closer to be heard over

the whistling wind, but her eyes stayed on the tall, commanding presence of Trystan bringing a well-known, friendly reporter into his discussion with Royce and the foreman. Good call. "I think you've all underestimated him. I'm honestly not sure he needs my help other than picking out clothes for special events, which you could have paid some-one far less to do."

Naomi laughed in a quick burst of disbelief. "Are we talking about the same man? The guy who hides out when there's any event with a guest list in the double digits?" Tapping her temple in faux concen-tration, she exclaimed with a slight edge, "Oh wait, that would be my fiancé."

Isabeau nodded, still focused on Trystan. Mag-netic charm pulled her in, seemed to make her feet ache to take even just one step toward him. "My point is that Trystan handles himself well with the press. He's in his element talking about issues per-taining to the land—like now. So the preservation fund-raiser capitalizes on his skill set."

"Are the press and protestors supposed to be coming in?" Naomi gestured to the news media and demonstrators that moved toward them, albeit slowly. Naomi pushed a hand into her back, stabi-lizing herself.

"We have a conference scheduled shortly. They are just setting up."

Although that was true, a wave of nerves pulsed

in her blood at the forward progression of angry people pushing at the simple orange tape barrier.

One. Two. Three. Four.

One. Two. Three. Four.

Isabeau counted through each breath in and out to subdue her nerves. The crowd's chants became louder, more urgent than before. Drums were added to the protestors' repertoire. She searched for Paige, and her dog seemed attentive but relaxed, which reassured Isabeau. Ignoring agitators, she turned her attention back to Naomi.

"Hmm," she said, absently fanning herself. Sweat crested on her forehead, discomfort contorting Naomi's mouth.

"How are you feeling?"

Naomi grimaced. "Fine."

"Are you sure?" Scanning the woman, Isabeau noticed other signs of discomfort. Naomi shifted her weight from foot to foot.

"I mean, I feel a little tired. But this wasn't something I could miss. Too big of a deal to leave to someone outside the family."

Another roar pulsed through the crowd. Protestors pushed through the barrier tape, banging their hands together, voices screechy. Panic mounted in Isabeau's throat.

"I can understand that. Perhaps a doctor's visit after this?" Her voice cracked, throat closing slightly as Paige whined and pawed in warning. The dog circled in agitation.

Surging forward, the gathering crowd closed in on them, drowning out Naomi's response. Panic fixed Isabeau to the spot. Colors and sounds faded, lost their vibrancy as the crowd jostled around them.

Light-headed, she could just make out the muscular build of Trystan pushing toward her. Shouting something she couldn't quite understand.

A protestor shoved into her, sending Isabeau stumbling back against Naomi. Paige let out a warning bark as the protestor advanced, and then the dog shifted her attention, body tense and alert as she raced back and forth between…Naomi and Isabeau? Barking and barking.

Had the jostling crowd and shouts confused Paige? Unusual, but Isabeau was struggling to process the mayhem. Dimly, she registered strong arms—*Trystan's arms*—yanking the protestor away from her right before…

Trystan punched the man square in the jaw.

Eight

Trystan knew he'd blown it.

Too bad he hadn't figured that out before he'd started swinging his fists.

But once Royce Miller and a security guard pulled him off the guy who'd been crowding Isabeau, the red fog of protective anger dispersed from Trystan's mind. The guard and Royce had quickly shuttled him into the site foreman's trailer, along with Isabeau, Naomi and a very agitated yellow Lab.

Once the door clicked closed, Trystan shrugged off the hands guiding—restraining—him. "I'm okay. I'm in control."

Royce eyed him skeptically, backing up a step and nearly running into a pull-down bed in the narrow Airstream. "If you're sure."

Trystan planted a hand on the built-in desk crowded with papers and calendars. His head throbbed with agitation. And worry.

"Absolutely." Trystan turned his attention to where it should have been all along—Isabeau. "Are you alright?"

He took in her pale face, her dog leaning heavily against her leg as she drew in deep breaths. His pulse still hammered in his head with concern for her.

"I'm shaken but fine." She stroked her dog's ears. "We need to think through how to spin this because the photos are going to be all over the internet before we even step back out." She glanced down at Paige. "Settle, pup-pup, settle."

The dog whined, tugging away from Isabeau, so unlike what Trystan had seen from the highly trained service dog. "What's going on?"

"I'm honestly not sure. Paige is giving the alert for diabetes, but I really don't think there's an issue for me right now."

Trystan shifted restlessly from boot to boot. "Should you check your blood sugar, to be safe?"

"I will, I will." Her forehead furrowed, and Trystan slid a bracing arm around her waist. "She's usually so focused on me. The only time I've seen her do this was back in the early days together. I was at a doctor's appointment, and she alerted to an older lady right before she suffered from diabetic shock—"

Naomi gasped, pressing her fingers to her lips, her other hand on her stomach.

Royce was by her side immediately, hand around her waist. "What is it?"

Naomi paled, a sheen of sweat on her forehead. "Paige was barking at *me*—"

Her words grew slower and slower, stretching out as if she were reaching for thoughts, for even the ability to speak, until she went completely still, pale and confused.

And ill.

Back at the compound in Naomi's old suite, Royce opened the fridge door, searching for fruit. He pulled out raspberry and mint leaves, placing them next to the small bowl filled with oranges.

He'd always been a man of routines, particularly in moments of stress and uncertainty. And damn. The events of the last twenty-four hours had pushed his limits, trying his well-tuned strategies. Starting with the oil malfunction and ending with his fiancée passing out after the altercation at the protest.

Protectiveness mobilized his movements after Naomi had zoned out. He'd barely registered the ride to the ER. He couldn't forget what the doctor had said. Naomi had gestational diabetes and needed bed rest to ensure her health and the health of the baby.

Pulling out a cutting board from the small kitchenette in Naomi's loft apartment in the Steele compound, Royce focused on what he could control. Like slicing perfectly sectioned oranges to add to the glass of ice water for Naomi.

The knife glided through the skin of the fruit, juice gathering on the cutting board, stinging the scratches on his hands from working on models as he continued to think through better safety features for the oil refining process.

He added two orange slices, four raspberries and a few mint leaves to the glass. Wanting to do more for Naomi. Knowing that she had reacted poorly to the news about bed rest. One of the reasons he adored her was for her streak of independence, her ability to take care of herself.

But the gestational diabetes scared the hell out of him.

The concern over her health and the twins' health took him back in time. To his former fiancée and her miscarriage. How she'd walked away. He'd lost everything. The pain of that breakup had haunted him ever since.

Losing Naomi?

The thought was more than he could bear.

He shuffled toward where Naomi stretched out

on the sofa. Nerves pulled at him and he was careful not to spill the fruit infused water.

He wanted to make everything easier for her. But he tried not to drive her crazy by hovering. Though if he had to be honest, he was halfway to going crazy too being stuck in this house full of Steeles and Mikkelsons.

So. Many. Damn. People.

Naomi slumped deeper into the sofa, tossing a magazine back on the coffee table. "Bed rest for gestational diabetes. Seriously." She reached down to pet their Saint Bernard, Tessie, sprawled on the floor by the couch. "I'm going to lose my mind."

"No, you're not." He gave her the glass of water and moved the remote control closer to her reach. "I'll keep you entertained."

"I enjoy you, don't get me wrong, but just the two of us—and Tessie—24/7? You may enjoy the life of a recluse, but it's not my cup of tea, at all." She took a deep gulp of water.

He stifled a wince at her grouchiness. Her frustration was understandable and she had to be scared. He just wished she hadn't mentioned how damn different they were, something that had been bugging him more than he wanted to admit.

"You have more family than anyone I've ever seen. Maybe you and your dad can share recliners in the sun."

She rolled her eyes, rubbing her stomach slowly.

"I'm not sure the world is ready for both of us to be tied down in the same place."

He chuckled softy. "Valid point."

Sighing with resignation, she said, "Go hibernate at work. Really. I'll be fine."

"I can work here." He forced an easy smile, even as the walls closed in on him. He gravitated toward the wall of windows showcasing the Alaska landscape…mountains, water, seclusion. He turned back to Naomi. "You might need something."

"I have a phone, along with a houseful of family and staff. I will be fine."

"But you're my fiancée."

"Then let's go to your place."

His place? Wasn't it *their* place?

"No…" He shook his head. "You're right that it's safer to be here at your father's compound, closer to town."

"I could be stuck like this until the babies are born. You would really live in the middle of all this chaos?" she asked, shock and disbelief stamped all over her beautiful face. "All these people?"

"For you. Yes." He meant it too, even knowing it wouldn't be easy. Already he was itchy, mentally listing places he could hole up on his own.

"But it's not in your comfort zone."

"It's not forever." He wouldn't let himself think about the idea of his isolated home making her feel as stir-crazy as this place made him. "Your health and the health of these baby girls is top priority."

Picking up her crystal water glass, she eyed him skeptically and stirred her straw through the fruit. "Okay, for now. Let's revisit this once we've recovered from the surprise."

"Sure," he said, not that he intended to back down. She needed to be here. He kissed her forehead, breathing in the scent of her shampoo. "Rest. I have work to keep me company."

"Okay, then," she answered, yawning, her eyes already at half-mast. "I'll be quiet…" Yawning again, she started to drift off in that near narcoleptic way he'd learned was common with pregnant women.

Exhaustion hit him hard and fast. Adrenaline letdown, no doubt. He eyed his computer across the room, but dropped into a fat recliner instead, snapping his fingers for his dog to join him. Tessie cast a soulful look at Naomi, then ambled over to him.

His heart turned over when he looked at Naomi, no question. He loved these two babies that—while not biologically his—were already his in all the ways that mattered.

But he was a man of logic and he couldn't ignore the hard, cold truth.

As he stroked the Saint Bernard's head, he couldn't help but think about how fast he and Naomi had jumped into this relationship. Their chemistry had been powerful; the emotions had run high.

They were in love long before realizing how damn different they were.

Now, watching her cradle her pregnant belly even in sleep, his heart turned over on itself. A new ache cracked open in his chest and he knew he wasn't going to be able to close his eyes and rest even though he was exhausted. She was starting to talk about how different they were.

How long before she decided the compromises were too great?

Isabeau drank in the Alaskan wilderness from atop a horse, hoping to figure out a way through some of the recent tensions. After taking Naomi to the hospital, they'd regrouped at the Steele compound.

Jeannie's home on the outskirts of Anchorage didn't have stables, so they'd opted to gather at the Steele mansion to confer with the family on the pipeline accident and the resulting press nightmare.

She'd sent out some social media messages that calmed the storm, or at least refocused the attention. Footage of an interview with Royce the day after the incident had certainly helped. He'd been surprisingly calm and collected during his scientific statement of opinion on the pipeline—despite his pregnant fiancée's health problems.

Now that Isabeau could catch her breath, she was struck again by how the sprawling Steele estate reminded her of an oversize—and far grander—log cabin, recalling the old days of Alaskan exploration. And as a light breeze cooled her skin, causing a flutter in the meadow grass leading up to the Steele compound, she felt as if they'd stepped back in time.

Trystan had given her a brief tour of the barn and an introduction to the horses. Even though he hadn't grown up on the Steele compound, she couldn't help but notice the way all the horses responded to him with perked ears and low whinnies. It seemed to her as if they recognized a kindred spirit. No matter that he'd lost his patience when he thought someone was crowding her, he was still the most even-tempered man she knew.

She fluffed the paint mare's mane, surveying the land and the horses that populated the pastures flanking the barn. Tucked in a field to the left, two massive draft horses chased each other. Mars and Jupiter, Trystan had said earlier. With their titan size and powerful haunches, they were inspiring. They seemed ethereal as they galloped, feet barely touching the ground in an awe-inspiring display. Thick manes and tales caught in the wind.

During moments like this, she felt like she understood Trystan's need to be away from the world of media and business. To sink into nature and horses rather than cameras and sound bites.

With a deep inhale, she rubbed the soft leather

of the reins, thankful for this stolen moment away from the media storm.

"The ride was a good idea. I feel more…zen now." Even if her thighs felt like liquid fire. Muscles she hadn't used in years were alive, awake. Reveling in the release offered by hoofbeats and country sky.

"Good, I'm glad to hear it."

"There's something timeless about unplugging from the world this way." Reaching down to the horse's shoulder, she dropped her reins, stretching as Willow the mellow paint stretched her long neck, letting out a low knicker as they approached the barn.

Trystan remarked from the flashy bay Abacus, "Interesting comment coming from a media specialist."

They walked a few more steps before Trystan stopped fifty feet from the barn. He slid off, dismounting with ease. She paused, taken by his natural grace and prowess with these creatures. Abacus stood at attention, ears alert and ready.

"I understand the importance of balance." At a slight tug on the reins, Willow stopped, patient as Isabeau adjusted her weight to dismount.

She paused, hand fixed on the horn of the saddle as Trystan approached, reaching for Isabeau. Her body slid down his in a long tempting glide. His strong arms held her suspended for a moment as they stared eye to eye, and then he eased her the rest of the way to the ground. "I'm sorry for losing my cool back there, but I'm so damn glad you're alright."

He angled down to kiss her. Or maybe she arched up. But his mouth covered hers in a perfect fit that was becoming increasingly familiar. It felt so very right, and that gave her pause, made her wonder what it meant. For her job? For her future in his life? She trusted him, but did not want that fist-throwing kind of staunch protectiveness around her. She'd become careful to rely only on herself.

But oh, how his mouth on hers tempted her to give in. Her toes curled in her shoes as desire spiraled inside her.

He stroked her hair and spoke against her lips. "I need to check in with the family."

"Do you want me to come along?"

"Not this time. We're going to talk mostly business rather than public relations. Take some time for yourself."

"Actually, I would welcome the chance to talk to Naomi."

"That would be helpful since maybe then Royce can be convinced to leave her side."

"We make quite a team."

He winked. "That we do."

A dark-haired stable hand approached, grabbing both Willow's and Abacus's reins. The horses la-

zily walked behind him toward the barn. Trystan
nodded his head, gesturing to the barn office where
they'd left Paige.

The yellow Lab greeted them with a rapidly wag-
ging tail and she happily trailed behind Trystan and
Isabeau as they made their way toward the house.

Trystan squeezed her hand, igniting butterflies in
her stomach. She pressed the button on the elevator
that would lead to Naomi's suite. When the elevator arrived, she felt reluctant to let his fingers go.

He flashed a deep smile at her as he dropped her
hand, striding toward the study where the families
were gathering.

She stepped into the elevator and pressed the
floor for Naomi's suite, along with the button for a
doorbell announcing her arrival. Isabeau fidgeted
with her hair, holding on to the feeling of his fingers twined with hers and the lingering sensation
of Trystan's kiss. Her stomach dropped as the elevator lifted.

The door dinged open, and she stepped out into
a room bathed in natural light. The high ceilings
and eclectic artwork suited Naomi's free-spirited
personality.

Her eyes stopped on Royce who hunched over his
computer at the small table. Earbuds in and zoned
out. Keys clicked in rapid succession, and she noticed the way his brow furrowed.

Naomi stretched on the light, airy sofa, chewing unenthusiastically on a celery stick.

Isabeau waved tentatively. "I hope you don't mind some company."

Naomi set aside her celery stick. "Oh Lord, thank goodness. I'm not even a day into bed rest and I'm going stir-crazy. So is poor Tessie."

Isabeau released Paige from her leash and gave the command, freeing her from work to enjoy herself. "Free play."

Tessie and Paige bounded over to greet each other like old friends.

Royce pulled his earbuds out. "Hello, thanks for coming up."

Isabeau said, "Trystan said to let you know they're having a meeting downstairs."

Royce closed his laptop. "Who is meeting?"

"Most of the Steeles and Mikkelsons, other than the honeymooners."

His shoulders heaved. "On my way." He skimmed a kiss along Naomi's forehead. "Take care of yourself." He opened the balcony door for the dogs to slip outside, then strode toward the small foyer.

Isabeau waited until Royce entered the elevator, doors closing him from view. She turned to Naomi. "Can I get you anything?"

"I'm fine. Royce has kept me well stocked with healthy snacks and fruit water. Would you like something?" She gestured to the coffee table that resembled a buffet with a veggie tray, pitcher of water and glasses. "Help yourself."

"Thank you." Isabeau poured a glass of sparkling fruit water for herself and sat in a recliner. "Are you okay? I don't mean to pry, you just have a worried expression on your face."

Naomi bit her bottom lip, releasing it slowly before blurting out, "I didn't want to upset Royce any more than he already is. But this experience has called back some upsetting times." She blinked back tears. "I'm a twin and my sister died in a plane crash when we were barely entering our teen years. This bed rest situation has made me think about her, like, all the time. If I sleep, I dream about her— Brea."

Isabeau didn't have siblings, but she'd loved her mother. Her mom—Loretta—had often worked two jobs, so time together was all the more precious. Sometimes her mother would even wake her up when she finished the late shift so they could talk. Loretta had never tired of telling bedtime stories, some of them fairy tales and some of them real-life histories. Such as the story of a famous Queen Isabeau, a strong woman with an elegant name.

Even now, there were times Isabeau dreamed her mother stood at the foot of her bed. Waking up to find her gone was devastating. Every time.

"I'm sorry." She touched Naomi's arm, squeezing lightly. "That must be difficult for you having all those feelings churning."

"It is." She rubbed her stomach absently. "She was taken from us so tragically."

Isabeau resisted the urge to touch her own stomach. Her period was a day late, which wasn't unusual, but still… She forced her attention back to the conversation. "Accidents can leave us with so little closure."

Her mother's death of COPD had given them time for farewells, but when her father died in a motorcycle wreck five years ago, there'd been no chance to figure out if the relationship could be repaired.

Naomi glanced out the window, lips pursed as she seemed to grow thoughtful. "At the time, there were rumors that it wasn't an accident at all."

"What do you mean?"

"The police could never prove anything, but there were unanswered questions and this pervasive sense that someone in the Mikkelson family had something to do with the accident."

Horrified and more than a little defensive on Trystan's behalf, Isabeau sat up straighter. "Oh my God, that's…unthinkable."

"Our families already disliked each other and some felt there wasn't room for both businesses in the industry."

"But to cause a plane crash?" She couldn't fathom such a thing.

"To keep from going insane with grief, I had to accept that I'll never know the truth." Yet, the pain of that decision still showed in her brown eyes. "And if someone tied to the Mikkelson business did it, they couldn't have meant for the outcome to be that horrific—maybe they intended a runway incident, fear, distraction in the family. I know, it sounds crazy but that was such a chaotic time."

"I can't envision your father letting go of the investigation." Jack Steele was a formidable force, even now recovering from the horseback-riding accident that had broken his spine.

The fact that he wasn't paralyzed? A miracle.

"Dad was devastated over Brea and my mother both dying. We hadn't realized how much he depended on Mom. Without her, he was just…lost. And then I got cancer and he stopped having anything to do with the business for over a year."

Isabeau thought of her own family, of her mother's grief over being abandoned. Over her struggles to build a life for them. Isabeau thought of her own possible pregnancy. Could she do this alone? Was she being hardheaded and impractical in keeping boundaries up between her and Trystan?

"How did you all pull through?"

"Uncle Conrad stepped in. He has his own business interests and this isn't his passion, but he's savvy and he kept things on track. We owe him so much."

"He isn't able to help now?"

"His own corporate interests have grown too large, and we're not children anymore. He says it's on us and he's right."

Isabeau couldn't help but note, "For a large family who says they want to keep the family business afloat, everyone sure is preoccupied."

"You have Trystan, who's more capable than he realizes, and there's my brother Marshall if you get desperate."

"What a ringing endorsement." They laughed together, a much-needed tension reliever. "And they're both so into the social scene. Not."

"Ironic. I get it. The only person more reserved than Trystan is Royce—and okay, maybe my brother Marshall, too, and he's been sent to a conference anyway—under duress. But at least he agreed to go. Family is everything to all of us— Steeles and Mikkelsons. It's what binds us. So much so that Trystan is willing to step way outside his comfort zone."

"So much so, Jeannie and Charles Mikkelson adopted their nephew." The story touched her heart.

"And my brother adopted Glenna's daughter, who isn't even her biological child," Naomi added.

"You are all lucky. You all have people to count on, no matter what."

As Isabeau spoke those words, she realized how applicable they were to her too. While she hadn't had the luxuries of this lifestyle, she had been fortunate too. From her mother to the older woman who had taught her how to crochet, to Paige…and even to Trystan.

The last realization stunned her.

She wondered how she'd allowed herself to become so isolated and independent since the stalker incident when actually she craved more connections. More family like these people had.

Perhaps a couple of weeks ago, Isabeau would have continued keeping him at a distance. But deep in her gut, she felt courageous.

She wanted to let her feelings carry her forward.

After a relatively successful meeting, and while the others had gone salmon fishing, Trystan found himself again craving the more familiar scents of horse musk, hay and leather.

The two former rival families turned business associates had meshed together better than he'd anticipated. Nothing like a string of crises to motivate teamwork and camaraderie.

Try as he might, the boardroom scene—with all its posturing—was never his thing.

But as much as he wanted to help his family, he was finding himself wanting to please Isabeau, as well. Still, before he spoke with her about the results of the meeting, he needed to ride off the tension.

And yes, give himself some distance from the attraction to Isabeau that was so strong he was beginning to lose objectivity.

Luckily, horses grazed just outside and he nodded his thanks to Royce before rushing to the barn, eager to exchange the wooden table and its complications for a pair of cross ties and Abacus, the spunky bay quarter horse.

He made short work of getting to the barn, clipping the leather lead line to the designer halter. Abacus's ears perked up as Trystan brought him to the cross ties. The horse stuck his tongue out in a lazy yawn.

After securing the bay, Trystan retrieved a tack box full of supplies. Picking up a currycomb, he allowed Abacus to smell it. The horse's whiskers tickled the palm of his hand. Once Abacus adjusted to the scent, Trystan placed a steady hand on the animal's neck, stroking the silky bay. With his other hand, he moved the currycomb in small, concentric circles, freeing some of the dirt and loosening Abacus's muscles. While he knew the stable hand had probably already done this, he felt peace of mind taking care of the horse himself.

From a distance, the now-familiar jingle of a dog's collar caught his attention. Looking over the bay's withers, he saw Paige keeping pace with Isabeau. His heart pounded just a little faster as he took in the red hair piled in a high ponytail on her head, the tight fit of her jeans and shirt.

Isabeau allowed Abacus to sniff her hand, stroking the other side of his neck. The horse leaned into the rub, clearly enjoying the extra affection. "Are you going riding again?"

"I'm just checking to make sure they were brushed and settled properly." He tipped his Stetson down, shaking his head. Trystan finished currycombing and picked up a hard, stiff brush.

"More decompressing after the family meeting?"

"Perceptive and pretty." He smiled over his shoulder, sending the tufts of loose hair and dirt off the bay's hindquarters. The excess hair and dirt pooled on the ground. "How's Naomi?"

"Settling in after her visit to the emergency room. It's reassuring they didn't hospitalize her, but she has gestational diabetes and elevated blood pressure. She's on bed rest."

"Gestational diabetes? How is that different from your kind of diabetes?" Placing the hard brush back in the tack box, he picked up a red hoof pick.

He'd needed their earlier ride to escape the pounding heat. He didn't want Isabeau to think he lost control at the drop of a hat after the way he'd punched that guy. But too many more tempting touches with this woman were going to drive him crazy.

Making his way back to the bay, he ran his

hand down the front right leg, touching the soft spot above the hoof. In a snap, Abacus responded, picking up his foot. With practiced ease, Trystan removed the dirt the horse had acquired from pacing in the stall.

"Yes, it's different. I had juvenile onset. It's a lifelong condition. Naomi's was brought on by pregnancy and should resolve after the babies are born. She just needs to take care of herself."

"And you're taking care of yourself…just in case?" He eased the horse's foot down to the ground again. A handful of flies buzzed around. Abacus swished his dark tail, shooing them away. The last flick of the tail smacked Trystan's shoulder as he moved to the right rear leg.

"Absolutely," she said without hesitation. "How did things go?"

He sighed, pleased with the cleanliness of the back hoof. "We're calling it a controlled disaster. No one was hurt, and nothing toxic happened to the land. So that's a win. But our major competitor is running with the story to push our stock value down."

"That's unfortunate, but not unrecoverable," she said as he moved quickly to the other two hooves, removing the dirt as she spoke. "You have some major positive events coming up with the fundraiser and Jack and Jeannie's wedding. Those will generate great airtime."

Setting aside the hoof pick, he dramatically gestured to his neck, faux gagging. "I can already feel the tuxedo bow tie choking me."

A sparkling laugh fell from her lips as she shook her head from side to side.

Damn.

The way the sun caught the bronzed hues in her hair made her seem like a mystical princess. She was so damn beautiful, generous.

As if she could hear his thoughts, a shy smile erupted as their eyes locked. Everything about her called to him. Closing the distance, the memory of how worried he'd been at the pipeline flooded him.

Trystan pushed those racing worries away, choosing instead to focus on the impossible blue of her eyes. Those lips parting slightly as he cupped her head...

And surrendered to the need to kiss her.

Nine

Isabeau couldn't deny Trystan's kiss moved her, always, and in ways no one else's kisses had before. Their connection was special, unique. She'd decided to take a risk, and here she was, forging ahead.

He backed her against the stall, the planked wall a welcome brace to keep her wobbly knees from giving out from under her. The weight of his body against hers anchored her, the heat of him warmed her inside and out. The scent of his aftershave mingled with the earthy musk of hay and animals around them. Combing her fingers through his thick hair, she wanted more of him. All of him. She couldn't hold out against his appeal much longer.

All the reasons they should stay apart felt elusive at the moment, only whispery thoughts about the way they grew up, of her need for self-reliance after an unhealthy relationship. Except nothing seemed to matter except the rightness of his arms around her. His mouth on hers.

A loud thud sounded through the barn, breaking apart their kiss, causing Isabeau to remember herself. Reverberations skittered in the air, and Trystan's protective arms seemed to shield her from the yet to be determined noise.

His gaze, which had been scanning sharply, softened as they realized the culprit. Jupiter—one of the draft horses—knocked into his stall's gate. An accompanying whinny following.

From across the way, his brother Mars peaked his head from the stall, neck stretching long as he bleated a response.

Isabeau's nervous heart stopped galloping, calmed as she took in the scene. Relieved, she glanced at Trystan, their easy laughs tangling as they relaxed, looking at each other.

Trystan pulled her close, a deep sigh forcing the breath from his lungs, causing his chest to dip in as she rested against him. He stroked her hair, his other hand low on her waist. "Why is it we never seem to find an extended private moment?"

"I'm enjoying myself here." She didn't want to

go back. Back to the real world with worries about if she'd done her job well enough.

"I agree, but I would like the time to linger over you and this place is too public. Anyone could burst in. While the media has us partnered up, I do not want risqué photos of you out there. I would never expose you to that."

His words warmed her, especially after having been with a man who was so untrustworthy. "I know. I do trust you to be an honorable man." And as the words came out of her mouth, she realized they were true. He was different from her father. He would never leave her and a child vulnerable.

Although trustworthiness wasn't the same as commitment.

"Things are moving fast. I get that, and you have to know that while I respect your wishes, I want more."

She appreciated his willingness to protect her from the media attention his family garnered, to give her space. Maybe it was time for her to give back, to take a risk.

Before she could second-guess herself, she plunged right in. "Between two brushes with the press, the world already sees us as a couple. Why should we deny the chance to see what's going on between us? Life could well force our hands soon enough."

"What do you have in mind?"

"I'm asking you out on a date." The moment she said it, she wondered if it sounded silly at this point. They'd gone everywhere together these past few weeks, spent nearly every waking moment together. But still. Was it so wrong to want a romance? A chance to really get to know him beyond their work relationship? The heated evening in the boathouse had happened with such fast intensity, they'd skipped over the milestones that usually came with dating.

"A date?" he echoed, his eyes intrigued, his knee brushing hers as he shifted.

"Just the two of us in a place away from the media, a chance to be together before the fundraiser and your mother's wedding." She watched him process the invitation while her pulse picked up speed.

Anticipating.

His gaze dipped to her mouth. Lingered. "I like the way you think." His voice did wicked things to her insides. "Did you have somewhere special in mind?"

"Surprise me." And she trusted that he would.

If only she could trust herself to keep her wits around him.

Royce wondered how a mansion this large could feel so damn crowded.

Since Naomi was settled with the other women

going over plans for the fund-raiser and reviewing details for Jeannie and Jack's wedding, he felt comfortable being away from her. Worrying about her blood pressure was exhausting.

He plowed through the kitchen, tablet under his arm, Tessie loping alongside. He would hide in the pantry with his work and his dog if he had to. Lord knew, their "cupboard" was as large as his dining room.

Head down, he slammed into—Trystan. "Sorry, man, I didn't see you." He gripped Tessie's collar. "Wait, girl, wait."

"My bad," Trystan answered, tucking his cell phone in his pocket. "I was wrapped up in finalizing a date night with Isabeau."

"A date night? So you two really have something going on, other than work," Royce said, to make polite conversation, something he was doing more of these days, being a part of Naomi's world and working for Alaska Oil Barons.

"I hope so." Trystan rocked back on his boot heels.

"Good luck to you." And he meant it. Relationships were tough. He had a failed engagement in his past to prove that.

"Thanks, I'm gonna need it. Unlike you, who already has your life all squared away."

"Uh, yeah."

Was that how he appeared? Didn't feel that way.

Hopefully, things would get back on track with him and Naomi once they could return to their cabin.

The sound of her laughter drifting down the hall halted that thought short, reminding him how happy she was here, with her family. Here, in the middle of a crowd.

Trystan clamped him on the shoulder. "Are you alright?"

"Sure, I just need to take my dog for a walk."

"With your tablet?"

Royce looked down. "Right, I was thinking Tessie and I could hang out on the dock, where it's quiet."

Trystan backed up a step. "Fair enough. I'll leave you to it."

Royce snapped his fingers for his dog to follow, then glanced over his shoulder at Trystan. "How do you handle being here, away from your ranch?"

Trystan rubbed the back of his neck. "I keep track of the days until I'm home again."

Not a reassuring answer. Nodding, Royce started toward the pantry, only to find teenage Aiden Steele raiding the shelves. "Want something?"

"No, thanks, I'm good." Shoulders braced, Royce redirected his path, aiming for the doors leading outside. He needed to get his head on straight and hunker down, keeping his priorities in order. Naomi and the babies.

He couldn't think too much about how what he

needed and what she needed seemed to be so different. Could he find peace with her? Could they really get along?

Could he fulfill his calling to save lives with his profession if he didn't have the space to work?

He did find quiet late at night, watching her sleep, his hand resting on her stomach to feel the babies kick. In those moments he could envision the future, hiking with the kids, taking sleigh rides, viewing the northern lights and teaching them about constellations.

Pushing open the French doors leading to the side yard, he drew in the fresh air. A warm breeze swept in off the water, carrying the sound of a cluster of Steele and Mikkelson men gathered on the dock, casting fishing lines. Their back and forth banter likely scaring away any fish. He pivoted away, eyeing the lengthy garage that held his truck.

Only a few more months until they could all return to the cabin.

So far, the evening was going exactly as planned. No media. No prying public. Just the two of them plus the faithful Paige at a secluded coastal restaurant, located on their flight route back to Anchorage. His plane and pilot's license were a must for his pioneer spirit, affording him the opportunity to explore his vast—and sometimes unnavigable—state.

Yes, he was trying to show Isabeau the wonders

of Alaska. She lived here, but he was aware this wasn't home for her.

And he was very aware that with every passing day, the chances increased that she was pregnant. It had been nearly three weeks since their impulsive hookup at his sister's wedding. As much as he wanted to ask Isabeau, he also knew that the longer the issue was unsettled, the more time he would have to persuade her to give them a chance to see where this attraction could lead.

He'd planned the evening to the last detail. And while he hadn't called his sister Alayna this time, she had inadvertently given him the idea to come here to Anastasia's by the Sound, with Russian-style food that they'd enjoyed growing up.

Gold gilded archways, deep walnut wainscoting, cream walls and linens accented with touches of scarlet in the artwork and napkins. The vibe here was elegant, like his dinner companion. Heavy gold candelabras graced each table, the white tapers flickering gently. Anastasia's pulled no punches on lush, romantic atmosphere and he hoped Isabeau would enjoy it.

They'd dined on smoked salmon, caramelized onion soup, lamb kebobs and coarse black bread. The conversation had been easy between them, carrying them to dessert before he realized two hours had passed. He'd forgone wine, unable to forget the possibility she was pregnant. They drank decaffeinated tea with citrus and vanilla and spices, along with a dessert of apple *sharlotka*—a mix of tart and cake.

But all the more enticing than any dessert?

Isabeau straightened across from him, the thin shoulder straps of her deep blue gown clinging to her curves. She wore a simple diamond necklace that caught in the muted light. Her pink lips parted in an easy, relaxed smile. Half driving him crazy as he imagined kissing her again, wrapping his arms around her while his fingers destroyed her loose curled updo.

How long had it been since he'd touched her the way he wanted to? Memories from the boathouse taunted him nightly.

Swallowing, he adjusted his body, feeling contained by the suit coat and tie. But it was worth it, if Isabeau was happy.

Her face was blissful as she tipped her ear toward the violinist playing the the famous song from Tchaikovsky's *Swan Lake*. Trystan winged a mental thanks to his mother that he recognized the tune.

Isabeau set her teacup down, candlelight reflected in her eyes and made her diamond pendant glitter. "Well, you absolutely did surprise me."

"What did you expect?"

"More local flavor, upscale sure, but somewhere with an Alaskan flair."

Sipping his water, he shrugged. "My parents

liked to travel. My sister Alayna was a huge fan of Russian food—which astounded us all because she was such a picky eater. Anyhow, that reminded me of this place where my family used to go when Dad was sick of her eating nuggets and pizza."

"Russian food. Go figure." She arched an eyebrow, her smile making him hunger for a taste of her lips.

"Well, it's closer than Moscow, plus the routes are crazy and then there's customs to deal with. Another time, perhaps. For now, this felt more…unexpected. You deserve to be romanced." He toyed with her fingers across the table, her pale pink nails and small silver rings feminine touches he appreciated.

"Impromptu travel usually makes me anxious, but you pulled this together so smoothly I'm completely relaxed." Paige snoozed under the table, a testament to the lack of need to keep watch for stress.

"Why would you say that about impromptu travel making you nervous?"

"I'm a planner. Knowing what's coming next soothes me." Isabeau drew absent circles on the tablecloth with her finger. "And I guess I thought you were a planner too. You strike me as a person who likes to stay on his ranch, even our trip to Juneau was familiar ground for you. That's the whole reason I was hired—because you don't like stepping outside your comfort zone."

"That's work. This is a date. Social is different from business."

"Hmm, interesting perspective. So you are a world traveler after all, like your family."

"Like them, but on my terms. There are so many places I would enjoy showing you. Denali National Park here in Alaska and viewing *Swan Lake* in London. Maybe even a trip to Moscow for authentic Russian food." He reached across the table and clasped her hand.

"Our time working together is coming to a close. The fund-raiser is coming up this weekend."

"I'm fully aware." The clock was ticking faster than the violin speeding through Tchaikovsky.

"And the following weekend is your mother's wedding."

"I'm *very* aware of that." Truth be told, his mother's marriage to someone who'd been their family's business nemesis still unsettled him. But, then, who was he to judge convoluted relationships? "It doesn't have to end there with us."

He stroked his thumb along the inside of her wrist, just over her speeding pulse.

"Whoa, Trystan," she said softly, squeezing his hand. "This is a date. Can we simply enjoy the moment and not discuss the future—other than preparing for the events?"

"Can do." He lifted their clasped hands and kissed her knuckles, savoring her creamy soft skin.

Then he raised his cup of spiced tea. "A toast. To your beauty, your charm and your compassion."

She relaxed back into her chair. Lifting her teacup, she clinked it lightly against his, then sipped. She eyed him over the rim of the fine china, her eyes...seductive. "Do we have a hotel for the night?"

His heart rate kicked up a notch to match hers, desire throbbing through his veins. "We can, if that's what you want?"

She smiled, slowly, deliberately. "I do, very much."

She was going to do this.

No backing down.

Isabeau intended to take every ounce of pleasure from this evening with Trystan that she could. She would store away the sensations and the memories for the future. She'd been through too many difficult times—had battled for her health and her independence—to turn her back on a chance to indulge herself with a man like Trystan. A man so thoughtful of her needs and desires.

Tomorrow would have to take care of itself.

Anticipation tingled through Isabeau every step of the way back to the five-star hotel on the rocky beach, waves crashing with romantic intensity. The golden elevator deposited them onto their floor, Trystan's arm around her waist, her head tucked against his shoulder. Her dog kept a step behind, seeming to sense this was a moment of privacy, that she wasn't needed.

His hand on the small of her back, Trystan maneuvered Isabeau deeper into the hotel room drenched in sultry hues. When she'd mentioned spending the night together, he seemed to pull a reservation out of thin air, taking her to a world-class hotel near the restaurant with the same decor. An overstuffed king bed heavy with crimson, yellow and deep blue throw pillows commanded the attention of the room. Bay windows caught the twinkle of the starlight above the water, deepening the romantic atmosphere.

She unclicked Paige's leash and took off her vest, giving her the command releasing her from work. "Free play." Paige trotted away, sniffing around the room.

Trystan's fingers slid from hers as he made his way to the dark wooden side table where an ornately carved incense holder was placed beneath a table lamp. He ignited a match from the nearby pack, the flame crackling as it took to the incense. Sandalwood flooded the room. He turned back around, an inviting look playing on his lips.

She reveled in sensation after resisting temptation for what felt like an eternity. Could it only have been three weeks since that night in the boathouse that had never been far from her mind? It seemed longer. Her body ached with wanting him.

She drew in bracing breaths to regain control, looking around the suite as he adjusted the heavy brocade curtains and placed his suit coat over a chair. He turned back to her, his eyes holding hers with a seriousness that touched her soul. He held out his arms.

And without another thought, she stepped into his embrace.

Her hands rested on his shoulders, her fingers curling into the warm starched cotton of his button-down shirt. "You said you wanted to linger, and that sounds quite…delicious."

She'd seen the stress on Naomi and Royce's relationship due to rushing things. She didn't want to face those same problems down the road if she and Trystan became…more. Better to really know one another.

"I like a woman who speaks her mind."

"Good, because communication is my thing."

"When I said I wanted to linger, that didn't exclude going fast, because we can follow with slow, and then slower."

"You're promising a lot."

"I look forward to hearing if you think I delivered."

"You're okay with my sharing my opinion? You're not…threatened by that?"

"I'm confident. And if something doesn't work for you, I will enjoy trying again and again to get it right." He dipped a kiss along her neck, the barest brush of his lips over her skin.

Tendrils of pleasure curled down her spine.

She shivered in anticipation. "That flows both ways. What do you want?"

His eyes lit with passion as he pulled her closer. "To watch you find pleasure. More than once."

Her breath caught. Not just at the sensual promise. But that he wanted pleasure for her. That he could put her first even now when they'd both held back for so long.

Her fingernails curled against the fabric of his shirt. "Considering how long we've been waiting and wanting, I don't think that will take long."

She hummed with sensation and they hadn't even peeled off their clothes yet. His touch was bound to send her reeling.

"Then, if I can add to my list of wants, seeing you naked ranks right up there." He kissed her temple, breathing the words lightly against her ear.

"Well that's easy enough to accommodate." She stepped back, keeping their hands linked.

"I want to help with removing your clothes." He tugged her gently.

She slipped her hands free and shook a finger at him. "I think my list of preferences tonight is that I watch your eyes…" she slid a thin shoulder strap of her dress down, revealing a strapless bra "…as you see me."

She shrugged the other shoulder free and shimmied the dress to pool around her feet, the satiny fabric whispered along her heated skin and made her all the hungrier for his touch.

His expression was ample reward and aroused her as much as she could see that she'd stirred him. His light blue eyes darkened to an indigo flame, the hottest gaze. It flicked over her, searing her with need. How had she denied herself—and him—this long?

He tugged at his necktie, making fast work of loosening the knot and pulling it off. He started on the shirt buttons and she sauntered forward, brushing his hands aside, freeing the buttons one at a time, her fingertips savoring the soft cotton of his undershirt.

Not that he was passive. He unfastened his belt buckle. She tugged his shirttails free and flattened her hands underneath, splaying her fingers along the heat of his skin. He was as deliciously muscled as she remembered, the planes and ridges of his body creating contours she longed to explore with her hands and lips.

Their hurried encounter in the boathouse had been so shadowy—intense—but without the time to get to know each other's bodies. He was right, they deserved to linger.

The word "linger" hummed through her mind and along her sensitized nerves.

His calloused fingers rasped over her skin to her back, unhooking her satin bra. A hiss of appreciation slid between his teeth a second before his hands slid away her bra and cupped the weight of her breasts.

Her reaction was immediate and intense, tingling tightness spreading throughout her. She told herself the feeling had nothing to do with pregnancy hormones. She was probably just late. Brushing aside the thought as quickly as it feathered through her brain, she refused to let it distract her from this moment she so desperately wanted to experience.

Then his mouth was on hers as they backed toward the bed until her knees bumped the mattress. They fell in a tangle of arms and legs and passion. The night was everything she'd fantasized it could be…and more.

The last of their clothing was swept away and sent sailing to the floor as they touched and tasted, exploring every inch of each other. Learning the plains and valleys of each other's bodies in the warm glow of the lamplight.

When her body reached a fever pitch, she whispered her need to him, urging him on. Trystan pulled a condom from his wallet and neither of them spoke.

He sheathed himself and stretched over her, propping up on his elbows to hold his full weight off her. She slid her heels up his legs, hooking her feet around his waist and pulling him closer, deeper, and… She lost track of her thoughts as he moved inside her. His fingers in her hair. His chest brushing against her breasts with each synched move of their bodies, which were fast becoming sweat slicked and flushed with rising tension.

Nipping his bottom lip and nudging his shoulder, she whispered her wish to be on top and he quickly accommodated, taking advantage of the opportunity to touch her more expansively. Then his hand drifted lower, lower still, to the core of her need, tempting and teasing her until her head flung back, her hair skimming her spine as—yes—she couldn't hold back any longer.

Her orgasm splintered in an explosion of sensation, a moan escaping her lips. Trystan rolled her again to her back and with a deep thrust, his hoarse cry of completion joined her sighs.

Bliss melted over her in the afterglow as they held each other wordlessly. As the passion cooled from her body, she listened to Trystan's rhythmic breathing beside her as he drifted off to sleep, holding her against him.

There was something so intimate about sleeping together, which sounded silly given all they'd just shared. But sleep was…vulnerable.

The warmth of his body and the softness of the sheets sent a chill up her spine as worry paced in her heart. Gazing across the dark room to the window, she focused on the stars. The roll of waves against the shore.

Rather than being a simple escape or offering answers, having sex with Trystan had complicated things for her.

Because she wanted more.

That shouldn't have been a big deal. It wouldn't have been if they'd simply met at a party, drawn to one another.

But the couples in their orbit reminded her too well of the problems they faced—a reclusive man, a woman who worked with those in the spotlight, the issues that came with children, and that didn't even scratch the surface of his convoluted feelings about family and her own anxiety over her father and stalker ex-boyfriend.

None of which she could change. She only had control over one issue and she couldn't hide from that any longer. Seeing Naomi's scare with gestational diabetes weighed on Isabeau. She couldn't ignore her late period any longer, especially not with health concerns of her own.

Once they returned to Anchorage, she would need to see a doctor to check on her diabetes— and find out definitively if she was pregnant.

Ten

Popping a smoked salmon canapé into his mouth at the Wilderness Preservation Initiative Fund-raiser, Trystan nodded as a gray-haired senator rambled on and on and on. Rather than focusing on the fusion of dill, smoked salmon and rye bread, he feigned interest, eyes widening at the appropriate moments. Ever so briefly, he let his gaze slide over the senator's sagging shoulder to Isabeau, watching her work the room with ease.

Listening well often passed as good conversation as far as the babbler was concerned. So Trystan ate and made all the right noises to keep the senator talking.

Chatting up the senator would increase the program's success, which was the purpose of tonight. And after the faux pas with the almost oil spill, making sure this initiative gained traction was essential to the company.

So yeah, while he had hours more face time with a slew of exhausting people, this event could make or break the newly merged company's image.

Shifting in his freshly shined boots—grateful Isabeau had relented on him wearing dress shoes— he smiled at the senator. The formal event called for a tuxedo, which seemed to restrict his range of motion. But Isabeau had picked out the clean-lined article of clothing, telling him he looked sharp.

In truth, he didn't see it. Isabeau, however, looked enchanting in her fit-and-flare gold gown.

In the crystalline chandelier light, she seemed to be of another time and place. She moved past him, catching his eye. She leaned a slender hand on the champagne-colored tablecloth, complementing the elaborate pale rose centerpiece.

Her strapless dress accented her bare collarbone. Red hair upswept in loose ringlets, mingling with the gold chandelier earrings. And damn. That smile on her perfectly pink lips turned him inside out.

She'd never looked more elegant.

Or more a part of this world.

Memories of their night together still seared through him. Their first encounter in the boathouse had rocked him, no question. But lingering over her, exploring each other? That surpassed anything he'd experienced.

He wanted more time with her, not just hours, but much more. Which he would have if she was pregnant. However, he wanted her to be with him because she wanted that as well, not because a baby tied them to each other.

Despite her anxiety, she worked the room with a glittering smile, Paige keeping close watch. He'd wondered how the attendees at this black tie event would react to the dog. But apparently the addition of service animals must be common enough among this set that no one paid other than passing attention.

Although he imagined it was also a nod to Paige's excellent training and Isabeau's seamless handling that allowed the animal to work without creating any sort of distraction.

He also felt somewhat at home here in the opulent penthouse ballroom of the Mikkelson Enterprises building. Unlike the Steeles' sleek and swanky office tower filled with conference rooms, the Mikkelson structure had a stately, refined presence absent of the contemporary fixation on chrome and clean lines. Both buildings were magnificent, but served vastly different purposes. The key to Alaska Oil Barons' success would be to use the appropriate location for each situation. When wining and dining needed to happen, the Mikkelson

Enterprises ballroom on the top floor was the clear winner. Part of the merger plan involved keeping both properties and capitalizing on the strengths of each one's appeal.

The harpist and string quartet on a large elevated stage provided a lilting melody, the notes seeming to complement the twinkling boat lights bobbing below in the harbor made visible through the window. A creamy white marble dance floor sported a few well-heeled couples leaning against each other.

Both families had showed up in full force—with spouses and significant others. All doing their part to engage the politicians and social elite. Even the head of their major competitor, Johnson Oil United, had attended. Cal Johnson loomed in the corner, sipping a glass of champagne.

A long shadow stretched over Trystan—the Steele patriarch and his soon-to-be stepfather, Jack Steele. "Senator, do you mind if I have a moment with my future stepson?"

"Of course, of course," the senator agreed, reaching for another glass of champagne from a silver tray being carried by waitstaff. "Great party, great party," he said in that conversational way some people had of repeating themselves. "I'm going to double my donation in honor of your incredible recovery from that riding accident."

Trystan eyed his future stepfather warily. Whatever he had to say must be important to break up a conversation with a political bigwig.

Jack pumped the senator's hand. "We're very grateful. Thank you." He gestured across the room. "I would steer you toward my lovely fiancée, Jeannie, and our media coordinator, Isabeau Waters. You'll be in good hands."

The senator clapped Trystan on the shoulder. "Nice job getting the message out, young man. Hope we'll see more of you."

With a nod, the man turned in search of Jeannie and Isabeau, Cal Johnson close on his heels. Having the competition on hand this evening could be concerning to some, but Trystan perceived a frustration in Johnson as the man saw the unity and great show of professionalism from the Mikkelson-Steele team.

Trystan nudged Jack. "Do you think we should rescue them from Johnson?"

Jack laughed, a deep rumble of sound. "Jeannie can more than hold her own with him. You should know that about your mother."

"I do, but I'm also her son, and you'll understand that Chuck and I have felt especially protective of her since our father died."

"I'm glad to know that. She's had a difficult time, and even realizing she's a strong person doesn't stop me from wanting to look after her."

"She deserves some peace." Trystan shifted uncomfortably.

"Having some trouble with the wedding still though, are you, boy?"

"I think we're all still surprised. Decades of animosity between our families can be tough to sweep aside—or rather it is for some of us."

"Understandable. We've slung some harsh words around over the years," Jack conceded. "I'm hoping we can put that behind us. Maybe someday you'll even join us for a family breakfast at Kit's Kodiak Café. It's a tradition I started with my brood when they were young. I would bundle them up quietly so their mother could sleep in…" His voice faded off at the mention of his dead wife.

"That doesn't sound like the Jack Steele my father told me about, the Jack Steele who fed small children to bears."

Jack laughed, full out and loudly. "You've got spunk in you. We'll find our way just fine."

"Good to know." And since Trystan wanted his mom to be happy and didn't have any choice but to accept this man in her life, he said, "I'll take you up on that breakfast when you get back from your honeymoon. But you're paying."

"Deal." Jack nodded curtly, then stopped Trystan from leaving by gripping his arm. "I want you to know that I love your mother."

"You've told us." Still he couldn't dodge the blindsiding swipes of memories of his father fuming in frustration over Jack Steele's business tactics. No tuxedo and profession of love could sweep away the fact that the guy had undercut his father, ruthlessly filching clients.

That history was a huge part of why Trystan had insisted on stepping into this business void for the month, rather than giving it over to one of the Steele offspring.

"And I'll keep saying it until you believe it," Jack said brusquely. "I appreciate you all putting on a good face for the merger."

Trystan half smiled, snagging a glass of champagne. This conversation was awkward as hell. "We don't have much choice."

"You could walk away. You have quite a portfolio of your own, more than enough to take over the ranch."

Trystan bristled. He refused to be shuffled aside when his mother needed him now more than ever. He was part of the family, and that wasn't something he would ever take for granted. "I owe my parents better than to turn my back on their legacy."

"That sort of loyalty is golden. You're my kind. For what my opinion is worth."

"Your opinion is important because you're important to my mother." He finished off his champagne and set the glass aside, his gaze straying briefly to Isabeau. "Although if you hurt her, my loyalty to you ends."

"I wouldn't expect any less." Jack tugged at his

tuxedo tie. "This thing almost has me yearning for the neck brace again."

The man's lighthearted way of referencing his near-death accident took Trystan aback, but also made him admire Jack a bit.

Jack Steele was as tough as his reputation.

And Trystan completely agreed on the tie issue. "I would suggest you ditch the tie and rest, but I suspect that would fall on deaf ears. So I'll just say, thanks for taking the time to reassure me about my mother."

"You're a good son." He squeezed Trystan's shoulder. "And I'm a perceptive old man who knows when a fella is distracted. Go dance with the media consultant."

A smile tugged at Trystan's mouth as he weaved around the elegant dinner tables, heart pounding as he made his way to Isabeau. Her arms crossed, highlighting her curves even more. She schmoozed with Miles, the owner of a fairly large news station. The wiry thirty-something-year-old leaned in close to Isabeau, scraping back his wheat-colored hair.

Trystan set his jaw, nodding as he closed the distance between them. "Thank you for attending tonight, Miles."

"Wouldn't miss it. The Mikkelson-Steele merger is big news around here. Our readers are pinning a lot of hope on the job creation of Alaska Oil Barons versus Johnson Oil." He cut his gaze to the side. "Although I'm surprised you invited Cal Johnson, him being the enemy and all."

Trystan cocked his head, sizing up Miles. "Is that a dig for a statement?"

"One can hope." Miles slid an arm around Isabeau in a way that felt a bit too familiar. "Your media maven here has been doing fine work sharing news about the conservation efforts of your company. That's going to cut into your revenue, though, and put you behind Johnson."

Trystan wasn't wading into that boggy interview territory—and besides, he wanted the bastard's arm off her. Now. "Isabeau works too hard. She's more than earned a dance."

In a swift motion, Trystan swept his hand into the small of Isabeau's back, hand sinking into the silky dress. Ushering her forward as the string quartet segued into a new piece…a Brahms waltz, too damn familiar from one of Alayna's long-ago violin recitals. With practiced ease, he spun Isabeau into his arms, her full-length gown swirling around her ankles.

Trystan folded Isabeau's hand into his, placing his palm on her waist. Having her in his arms again felt good, right, easing some of the awkwardness that had crept between them when they woke up in the hotel the next morning. Awkwardness made worse when he'd tried to broach the subject of her seeing a doctor.

She'd changed the subject and taken her dog for a walk.

He opted for neutral territory now. "How am I doing tonight?"

She squeezed his hand lightly, smiling. "You're acing everything and you know it."

"I haven't hit anyone. That's a bonus. Although I was hard-pressed when that news producer put his hands on you." He drew her closer than the waltz stance dictated.

"I appreciate your restraint. And the board of directors and investors will be pleased. Any jitters should be quelled. You've all presented a unified front. The wedding next weekend will only solidify that."

Her every word was perfect. Her dance moves smooth. But now that he held her closer, he could see a distance in her eyes, a distraction.

Something was wrong. And if the past was any indication, getting her to open up wouldn't be easy. Not that he was the poster boy for baring his emotions.

Except right now he wanted to know what she was thinking more than he could remember wanting…anything.

Just as he lined up the right words, the music ended and with a tight smile, Isabeau stepped back to walk away.

Fading into the crowd.

* * *

Contrary to her carefully chosen outfit and permanent smile, Isabeau felt the cool hands of panic
wrench around her heart and she had no recourse
for relief. She'd sent Paige with a driver a half hour
ago as the party ran long. Luckily, the Steele stable
hands that looked after Kota had taken to Paige.
Her dog had already worked a full day, and Isabeau
thought she was holding her own.

Apparently not.

The Herculean task of keeping it together frayed
her nerves. A scene from earlier today played on repeat in her mind, drifting through her mind's eyes
in flashes. The waiting room, the doctor handing
her information about what to expect when you are
expecting.

The test was positive. They'd even done an ultrasound because of her diabetes, along with a slew
of other tests.

She was healthy. And her concerns about anxiety
medication had been discussed. She hadn't taken
much since the night she'd slept with Trystan, and
the two times she had, the medication was on the
approved list.

The doctor had mapped out a health care plan
for her to take with her when she left. And didn't
that thought launch a fresh wave of nerves and her
first hint of nausea.

Focus. Breathe.

She tried to take comfort in the fact that she knew, deep in her heart, that Trystan was not even remotely like her stalker ex-boyfriend. But she was just so damn scared of ending up like her mother, in a relationship with a man who would walk away from her.

She had to admit the truth to herself. She already loved this baby.

And she was starting to care for the baby's father.

Isabeau needed a breather from the whole party. How ironic that Trystan was mastering every obstacle, and she was on the edge of losing her cool. Her life had been turned upside down so often since she'd met Trystan, she wasn't sure yet how to right herself.

In a dimly lit back corner, Isabeau found something that looked like salvation. A secluded spot where Naomi sat on a chaise lounge, putting her feet up. Her dark hair had been styled pin straight, evoking the unearthly beauty of Cleopatra. She looked the part, lying on the chaise in her high waisted Egyptian-style, green satin gown, the hem trailing off the side. The gown was clingy and exotic, and somehow the pregnant woman carried it off beautifully. Even in her second trimester—with twins.

Jeannie was sitting beside Naomi, chatting, keeping her water glass full.

Isabeau backed up a step. "I'm sorry for interrupting."

Naomi set aside her glass. "Not at all. Jeannie's been a love to keep me company—lounging here is as much excitement as the doctor will allow me. While I'm glad to be out of my suite, this certainly isn't the most fascinating part of the party."

Jeannie patted her hand. "Those are Jack's grand-babies. It's a delight to talk to you about plans. And hopefully the doctor will give the okay for you to have a baby shower."

Naomi scratched her nose. "I can't believe I need a doctor's approval to open a few presents. I would offer to send Royce in my place, but as you can see from his ghost act a half hour into the event, crowds are not his thing. Quite frankly, I was surprised he didn't stay to hover—which attests to how really pegged out he was."

Isabeau sat at the foot of the chaise, perched on the end. "Trystan doesn't care for them, either. There's no shame in that."

Naomi pointed toward the party. "But Trystan showed up and, judging by what I can see from here, he's making the best of the night."

Jeannie followed her gaze, smiling fondly. "I have to say I'm proud of the way my son has come through for us. Due in no small part to you, Isabeau."

Isabeau smoothed her dress along her knees, the reality sinking in that this woman was the grand-mother of her child. "You did a wonderful job bringing him up and giving him the tools to work with. I fully expected to have to teach him about classical music and how to dance. But, well, he surprised me."

"Thank you, dear," Jeannie said, pride shining from her smile, and then she reached to clasp Naomi's hand. "It'll work out, for you, Naomi. You and Royce are different, but it's clear you love each other."

Naomi twisted her engagement ring round and round. "He loves the babies so much, which trust me, warms my heart. He thinks of them as his own even though he's not the biological father. And he's already lost one child…"

Jeannie leaned in closer, patting her shoulder. "Honey, are you saying you don't love him? Because if you are, you can't stay with him for the children."

Those words certainly chilled Isabeau to the core.

Naomi smoothed her hands over her pregnant belly. "I don't know what I'm feeling anymore, and I'm not sure he does, either. Everything moved so fast with us. We barely know each other, and what we do know seems less and less compatible now that, um, now that we're not relying on sex to smooth over the rough patches." She glanced up. "Isabeau, I hope I'm not making you uncomfortable."

Her worry about her own situation must have shown in her face. She smoothed her features into sympathy. "I'm the soul of discretion, and I've become quite fond of your family. While I don't have advice to offer, I can always lend an ear."

Naomi played with her dark hair, looking at her future stepmother through the strands. "Jeannie? Do you have thoughts?"

"I think you have to decide what's in your heart."

"You have to know me well enough to realize I'm not the vulnerable type to go around asking for help. I have opinions on everything. Usually." Naomi glanced at her hands, then looked up with a hint of embarrassment in her eyes. "I wish I could ask my mother." Then she rushed to add, "I hope that doesn't hurt you to hear."

Jeannie's eyes grew soft. "Of course not. That's a logical wish, especially now." She drew in a deep breath. "I'm not your mother and I can't begin to guess at where your feelings should or shouldn't land. But I can say this. If you're going to make a break, it's better to do so before the twins get attached."

Tears leaked down Naomi's cheeks and Jeannie gathered her into a hug.

The wisdom in Jeannie's words scared Isabeau to her toes, while also making her next move crystal clear. She needed to decide about a relationship with Trystan now. For the sake of her future, for her child. She didn't have the luxury of time to wait and see how things played out, risking a horrible breakup later when there was a baby in the picture.

She eased away from the two women quietly. She couldn't wait for another ultrasound. Trystan deserved to know now.

She searched the fund-raising event for Trystan. Eyes scanning the teeming crowd, looking for the rugged cowboy in a tuxedo. He carried the tux well, clean and sharp lines accenting his broad chest. Trystan gestured with his hands as he spoke with Jack Steele, Delaney and key donors.

Heart thundering as Isabeau looked at the scene, her racing thoughts anxious for the future.

As soon as the evening wound down, Isabeau was going to ask Trystan to take a walk.

They needed to talk.

Of the many uncomfortable moments of Naomi's life, the ride in the limo with Royce—after that honest conversation with Jeannie—seemed to top the list. She'd finally found him by calling him on the phone. Twice.

He'd made his way to the limo. Waited inside with a vacant look settling onto his dark features. He'd given a small smile when she'd slid into the leather seats.

Silence lingered between them, feeling as heavy

as a thick Alaskan blanket. The limo lurched forward and still no one spoke.

Even after Jeannie had given Naomi the impetus she needed to talk to Royce, she couldn't convince her tongue to form coherent words or thoughts. An ache weighed heavy in her chest as the limo turned the corner, the dim boat lights fading from view.

She couldn't go on like this. *They* couldn't go on like this.

Naomi broke first, tension mounting in her jaw. Another ache. Another result of feelings that she didn't know how to articulate. So she started simple. No flash. Just an honest statement.

"I missed you during the fund-raiser."

Royce tugged his tuxedo tie off and pitched it to the floor, his gaze dropping. "I wanted to have the car ready. You've been overdoing it tonight."

Indignation zipped through her, making her all the more irritated and uncomfortable. "My doctor okayed my attending this event."

"He didn't say you could go hiking."

"I wasn't hiking." She pulled her shoes off before he noticed the swelling. "I was sitting on a chaise."

"It was quite a haul up there," he said, head leaning against the glass. Royce tapped his fingers, which grated on Naomi's nerves.

"No one has suggested I should use a wheelchair. And if you're so concerned, maybe you could have stuck around instead of playing the hermit," she barked tersely, crossing her arms over her chest.

"The crowds got to be too much for me. I put in an appearance the way anyone would expect a member of the company to do."

A deep breath. Then another.

She looked out the window, eyes taking in the streetlights that illuminated tall pine trees and glinted off street signs. Of course, Naomi barely registered these things. Unease spread through her chest, forming knots in her shoulders and adding to the lump in her throat.

Jeannie's advice knocked around inside her brain as it had for the past two hours, coalescing all Naomi's doubts. She knew Royce would never walk away from her— most certainly he wouldn't walk away from the babies. But was she pushing him into a life that would make him unhappy? She certainly couldn't commit to a life in the wilds out of the public eye. So how could she ask him to force himself to "put in appearances" in her world full of people and family?

She twisted her engagement ring again, checking to make sure her fingers hadn't swollen too much, something she found herself doing more and more often as if she already knew she might need to remove it for a heartbreaking reason.

"I think we rushed into things."

He sat up straighter, his jaw jutting as the chauffeur drove through the security gates outside the

Steele family compound. "I disagree. We simply moved fast because we know our minds."

"Do we? We're almost strangers in many ways."

"Then tell me what you want me to know," he said in a clipped voice as if compatibility could be as basic as filling out a history profile.

"It's not that simple and you have to see that. I've had complicated relationships because of what I experienced in the past, losing my mother, my twin sister, battling cancer so young." She stared at her home, a place of such joy and loss. Part of her wanted to run, now that the car had stopped, but she had to see this conversation through. "You've had a challenging time with relationships in the past too—and that was with someone you'd known nearly your whole life."

He took her hands, irritation fading to concern in his dark eyes. "I think you're scared of what we feel."

"I know that I'm feeling smothered and over-whelmed."

"You're pregnant with twins." His voice cracked with pain.

Twins, the babies. Children he wanted. But not the right reason for them to build a future together, especially when he and she already had such differing lifestyles. She feared she was being selfish by hanging on to him when she knew how restless and unhappy he was in her chaotic world.

"And I'm grateful that you care. That's sweet and I know I should count myself lucky, but I'm more concerned about our very different natures. You're a lone wolf and I'm a social butterfly."

"A steely butterfly."

Right now, she felt anything but steely. That would have to come later. After she'd gotten through the deepest hurt she'd ever felt. And considering all she'd already lost, that was saying a lot. She drew a ragged breath.

"Okay, but you have to see our lifestyles don't blend. Even trying to split our time between living your way and mine is already wearing thin. Ultimately, we'll each just end up miserable half of the year."

"I can see you're worried. Get some rest, and we can talk about this lat—"

"All I've done is sleep. You're not hearing me, Royce." Her throat clogged on tears for a moment, but because of how deeply she cared for him, how deeply she cared for her unborn children, she had to let him go. "Royce, I'm breaking things off."

She tugged free her engagement ring, a ring that had made her heart sing just not so long ago. But even as she accused him of being a hermit, she'd been hiding from the truth.

She placed the ring into his hand and closed his fingers. "Please, let me go."

When she pushed the car door open, Naomi

caught sight of Trystan and Isabeau taking a walk on the Steele grounds—why weren't they at the Mikkelson place? A question that she shoved aside because right now all that mattered was support she so desperately needed. Locking eyes with her new friend, she registered the distress and unease swimming in Isabeau's eyes. A distress and unsettled feeling that reverberated in Naomi's own chest.

Collecting herself, Naomi bolted from the car, moving swift and sure before Royce could intervene.

Eleven

Gray clouds speckled the night sky as Trystan reached for Isabeau's hand. They'd come to the Steele compound to pick up Paige, then he'd impulsively asked Isabeau to walk first along the shoreline She took his hand gingerly, though her slender face stayed fixed on the rocky shoreline in front of them, Paige off-leash enjoying free time to play.

They began to meander on the shoreline, maneuvering away from the house. He hoped to use this time to persuade Isabeau to see a doctor, to end this limbo state so they could move their relationship forward with direction—either way, baby on the way, or no baby.

Dropping his hand, she stopped walking. In the distance, he could make out the form of the seaplane.

Trystan shot her a sidelong glance, watching the moonlight find purchase in the lines of worry set in her cheeks and brow. "You said you wanted to walk. Is everything alright?"

She drew in a deep breath, stopped, turning to face him. "There's no simple way to lead into this. I saw the doctor, and she confirmed that I'm pregnant."

Her words hit him right in the gut. He'd been expecting it, thought he'd prepared himself. But *possibly pregnant* was nowhere near close to *really pregnant*.

Thoughts tumbled over one another in fast succession. Where would they live? How could he make her happy? When was the baby due?

She was carrying his baby.

His. Baby.

Isabeau held up her hands and turned away, walking again. "Never mind. No need to say anything. We can talk later once the news has sunk in."

She hitched her formal gown up past her elbows and started trekking back toward the house. Damn it. That wasn't how this conversation was supposed to happen. He was supposed to have some suave words to win her over.

"No, wait," he called out, grasping her arm. His bare feet desperate for traction on the muddy shore. "We should talk now. Keep in mind, I'm not good with words—as you know—and I want to make sure I get things right."

She glanced back over her shoulder, chewing her bottom lip, but staying silent. The moonlight brought out the gold in her red hair—and illuminated the fear in her eyes. "I'll be fine. The baby and I will be fine. I just wanted you to know, and now that you do, I'm going."

Crickets hummed, adding another layer to the sound of the rhythmic waves. Paige darted by them, splashing. A momentary distraction.

He needed the right words. "Isabeau, I should have my thoughts together on what to say. I've certainly thought about this possibility often enough over the past four weeks. One thing is clear though, I'm here for you and the baby." He pushed forward with what he knew was the right thing to do. "We'll get married. I'll take care of you, there's no need to be anxious. And my child will never have to feel abandoned or unloved."

No child would go through what he had when his parents dumped him, leaving him confused as hell trying to make sense of how a parent could just opt out.

She exhaled, her forehead furrowing. "I hear that you're trying to do the honorable thing, and that's… admirable. But I'm having trouble wrapping my head around how you said, 'No need for me to feel anxious?' You want to marry me so I won't have a panic attack?"

"That's not exactly what I meant." But he could see he'd offended her. He was making things worse the more he spoke.

She moved over a large rock formation, swaying slightly beneath the slippery surface. Instinctively, Trystan's hand shot out to steady her. Anger colored her cheeks as she shooed away his help, stabilizing her footing without him.

From her perch, her frown deepened, her voice becoming as dark as the night sea. "I thought you understood about my anxiety." The wind plastered her dress to her slim body. "But I'm wondering if you think I'm a needy person incapable of taking care of myself."

Hands extended in protest, he tried to steer the conversation back to more even ground. "That's not what I meant at all. You're clearly one of the most competent people I've ever met."

"What did you mean, then, with the anxious comment?" She crossed her arms. The moonlight fell on her, made her appear to be a living flame in that gold dress with her red hair.

"I just want to make life easier for you and the baby and, yes, I want to be with you. You and I have great chemistry. We enjoy each other's company. Marriage between us could be good, very good. Just think of all the bucket list items we could explore together."

"Bucket list? Bucket list?" Her voice pitched higher with each word. "We should get married to check off bucket list items together?" She shook her head. "Trystan, you can get a pal to do that. Marriage is—should be—about something else. It should be about love, and you don't love me."

Hell. He should have thought to use that word because he did care for her. "We have feelings for each other. I think with time that could—um, will—grow into love."

Her mouth thinned, anger radiating from her. "Trystan, you really should stop talking because you're making a mess of this."

"Then tell me what you're thinking since you're better with words."

"I believe you're offering marriage because you're still trying to make the perfect family, and that's not a reason for us to be a couple. Please be honest with yourself."

Her words sparked frustration and, yes, anger in him. He held his voice in check and said tightly, "You want me to be honest? How about this? I'm not sure you could love me even if we were perfect for each other. You hold yourself apart from people. You're too afraid of losing your family again—whether it is because of your father walking out or your mother dying—to take a risk on what could be a really good thing."

She blanched, her face pale in the moonlight, her eyes shining with unshed tears. "Then I guess we know where we stand and it's not together."

Turning away, she walked down from the rock, landing in the sand with a slight thud. Without looking at him, she walked past him. Away from him. Leaving him with nothing but the cold truth.

He'd done what he'd vowed he would never do— alienated his baby's mother. Anger at himself battled with a sorrow deeper than he could have ever imagined.

The last time Trystan had been up in the middle of the night raiding the kitchen, he'd been a teenager. But here he was, on his way to rummage for food, restless.

Five days had passed since Isabeau gave him the boot. Five days of tense work exchanges as she spelled out the tightly contained media exposure for Jeannie and Jack's wedding. Everytime he tried to bring up making plans for the baby, she insisted that could wait until the second trimester.

Which meant months of the cold shoulder.

And he didn't have a clue how to win her back. Desperation gnawed at him. He felt the weight of being orphaned all over again...his whole life and outlook shaped by the abandonment of his parents. He wouldn't allow his child to feel that. He couldn't. He wanted to be with Isabeau, to try, but she was right that the stakes were higher with a baby involved and nothing short of love was fair.

Except how were they going to figure out if that was possible if she'd shut him out?

Weighed down with regret, he made his way toward the kitchen, his feet slowed by the knowledge of all the ways he'd screwed up. He hadn't slept in days, and staying in his room staring at the ceiling wasn't going to help.

He turned the corner, surprised to see the kitchen aglow. His mother sat on a stool, hair in a messy blond bun. Deli meats and cheeses covered the lava stone countertops. Sliced bread, lettuce, tomato and onions flanked the sandwich supplies. Perhaps most notable in the sleek white kitchen with stainless steel accents was the opened gold-labeled Icecap Brews beer bottle in Jeannie's left hand.

"Hi, Mom, trouble sleeping? Wedding jitters?" The rehearsal dinner was tomorrow, the wedding the next day. He would have no date—no Isabeau—the spot beside him vacant.

"No nerves, dear. I'm sure. I'm just unsettled about other matters. The news about Naomi and Royce splitting up caught us all by surprise. Jack is beside himself worrying for his daughter." She nudged the sandwich makings toward him so he could make one for himself.

The breakup gave him pause too, as if he didn't already have enough reasons to wonder about his own relationship with Isabeau. How did he stand a chance winning her back when a perfect couple like Naomi and Royce couldn't make it work?

And there was still the baby to consider. They

would be connected through the child forever, and while he wanted the baby, the thought of making polite arrangements with the woman who'd just stomped on his feelings made his head pound—his chest ache.

Grabbing for the rye bread, he loaded the sandwich with roast beef, turkey, pepperoni and Swiss cheese. Losing himself in routine to keep from thinking about how much he hurt.

Jeannie finished chewing, scrutinizing him. Reading him, just as she'd done when he'd been much younger yet every bit as lost. "Is everything alright?"

"I'm just hungry. Can't sleep when my stomach's growling."

She picked up her sandwich and leaned against the counter. "You used that excuse as a child to keep from going to bed."

"When I visited here." He chuckled at the memory of those summers spent with his aunt and uncle—now his parents. "I'm surprised you remember."

"*Visited*...what a strange word. When I think back to those times you were here as a child, in my mind they're not visits anymore. They're...memories of my son."

"I appreciate your saying that."

"I mean it." She reached out to squeeze his hand, intense eyes burning into his. "You're mine."

"But I wouldn't have been if my biological mother hadn't been such a loser. You would have stayed Aunt Jeannie."

"If, if, if." She waved her hand as if she cleared the air of smoke. "That doesn't matter. I think in terms of 'what is.' And you were destined to be my boy. So, son of mine, what's wrong?"

He weighed whether to tell her. He didn't want to add more worry to her wedding week. He started to deny any problem, but he saw the determined look in her eyes, an expression he recognized well. She wasn't going to give up.

He took a bracing swig of beer, then admitted, "Isabeau's pregnant."

"Pregnant?" She set her sandwich down slowly. "I did not expect that. Although maybe I would have considered the possibility of you two as a couple if I wasn't so distracted these days. You two have been rather…cozy. So that means…"

"Yes, the baby is mine."

Smiling, she opened her arms. "Congratulations. Becoming a grandma is wonderful news…" She paused, her arms falling to her sides. "But you're not smiling."

Because his plans for the future were in tatters. His hopes for a future with Isabeau, gone.

"She turned down my proposal. She said I don't love her and that I'm only trying to create the perfect family my birth mother wrecked."

"Do you feel there's any truth to that? Do you love her?"

Love her? He exhaled hard. "Mom, how the

hell would I know? I just know I'm wrecked at the thought of living without her."

Jeannie's eyebrows pinched together in the worried mother look she'd worn more than once over the years. "How do you know? I can't tell you what you feel. I can just say that I've fallen in love—and been loved in return—twice in my life. Both times were different. Your father was my high school sweetheart, a love that builds over years, a love that matures together. With Jack? It was more like a blindsiding of emotion. A lightning strike when he walked into a room and I saw him with fresh eyes, knowing that my life would never be the same in a very good and amazing way." The worry lines smoothed, her eyes wise. The wisest he'd ever known. "Trystan, Isabeau looks at you with that 'struck by lightning' look. Make your decision and treat her heart with care."

Her words cut through him, the thought of hurting Isabeau paining him worse than his own heartache. The beginnings of a revelation that would change his world… He tried to smile, to make light of the revelation because having his world change so drastically wasn't totally comfortable. "I thought you would be on my side."

"I am. Always. I want you to be happy. You're my son and I love you. Unconditionally." She reached to cup his cheek. "I have to confess though, I would hope you felt you had the perfect family here with us. I know that Charles and I found our family to be finally complete once you became ours."

Guilt tweaked at him over her words and the sense that he might have hurt her. "Mom, you know I love you."

"I do know that, son."

Son.

He'd heard the word from her a million times, but right now, for some unknown reason, it resonated. Deeply. Instilling peace and confidence in him to face what was right there waiting for him.

He was Jeannie and Charles Mikkelson's son. He'd had the perfect family as their son—he still did.

And now it was time for him to build a family with Isabeau. The woman he loved.

Yes, loved.

He just prayed she loved him too.

Her heart still raw from her breakup with Trystan, Isabeau wondered how she would make it through this Mikkelson-Steele wedding without bursting into tears. But she was here, as per her job, and she would hold herself together with the help of Paige at her side.

Isabeau snuck a peek into the church, drinking in the lightness of the oak pews and the rich colors filtering in through the enormous stained glass windows. Arrangements of orchids and stephanotis lined the aisles of the church, elegant and, yes, fairy tale–like.

Her eyes blurred with tears over that other wedding a month ago, how the fairy-tale feel had tempted her so.

The *man* had tempted her.

The day had led to one of the most memorable evenings of her life with Trystan. The evening they'd conceived their child.

Absolutely breathtaking.

Her heart pounded, nerves getting the better of her even with her Lab leaning against her leg. She'd been invited to the bridal room before the ceremony. Things had been…tense over the last few days. And that was putting it mildly. But she'd promised to see this job through to the end.

Which was how she wound up at Jack and Jeannie's wedding *and* in the bridal room with all the women in the family. Jeannie's daughters, her daughter-in-law and her soon-to-be stepdaughters flanked her, forming a semicircle around the bride. Her lacy tea-length gown was bespoke elegance.

Jeannie's light blond hair was streaked with moonlight gray, making her seem ethereal. Especially since her hair was gathered into a French twist with embedded baby's breath and peonies.

No doubt, Jeannie Mikkelson was a stunning woman. But she wore joy as visibly as her pearl-and-diamond earrings and necklace. Truly, the blissful expression on her face became her most beautiful accessory.

With the skill set of a conductor, Jeannie moved her hand across her body, gesturing for the conversation to fade. As commanding as she was beautiful.

"Girls, my dear girls, I want to thank you all for being here today to celebrate. I realize this wedding could have been something to divide a family, but it means the world to me how you've all come together. My girls, to support me. Jack's girls, to welcome me."

Glenna Mikkelson-Steele, the oldest daughter, stepped forward. "Jack's accident was a wake-up call for all of us about what's important. Family. Love. Unity."

The other daughters and the daughter-in-law, Shana, all nodded in agreement. Even Naomi nodded, resting on a floral sofa with her feet up, her eyes swollen and red. Isabeau had hoped the woman's breakup would blow over, but it didn't appear that was the case. Happiness could be so fleeting.

Jeannie tucked a stray hairpin back into her chignon. "This love caught me by surprise—"

Glenna laughed. "I bet you weren't nearly as surprised as Broderick and I were to find you two in the shower together at work."

As the others giggled, Isabeau clapped a hand over her mouth. That little nugget of gossip had never made it to the press. Even Paige tipped her head to the side with an inquisitive expression in her wide brown eyes.

Jeannie leveled a *look* at her daughter. "My point

being, love can be in the last place you expect to find it. You could so easily miss it if you aren't open to possibility and compromise." She toyed with her diamond-and-pearl necklace, an engagement gift from Jack Steele. "Alright, enough with speeches and sage advice. I wish you all a lifetime of joy, my dears, and look forward to celebrating every precious moment with you."

Isabeau held back while the daughters hugged Jeannie, all careful not to smudge her makeup or muss her hair. Then as they dispersed, Isabeau leaned down to pass Jeannie the *something blue* handkerchief. "Thank you for including me in your group here."

Jeannie squeezed her hand. "Thank you and Paige for joining us. And thank you for all you've done to help our family, and Trystan in particular. Your work has made this day all the more worry-free."

"I'll miss you all when I go." Her throat went tight, and Paige nudged her.

Jeannie's grip tightened on her hand, her eyes probing. "I wish you didn't have to go. You fit in quite nicely with all of us."

Isabeau froze. Had Trystan told her something? This certainly wasn't the time or place to ask. But if he had, then Isabeau could swear what she saw in Jeannie's eyes was welcome, acceptance. And a familial warmth.

It had been a long time since Isabeau had felt that, and on a day when tears were already so close, the feeling speared deep into her heart. "Thank you. It's been an honor to be a part of helping along a wonderful family."

Except she wouldn't be cut off from them completely. Soon they would all know about the baby. All the women in this room would be a part of her life—of her child's life.

As the beauty of the love in this family wrapped around her, she realized how very much she wanted it—not just for her baby, but for herself.

How much she wanted Trystan's love, because she had fallen deeply and fully in love with an incredible man. And if she wanted a chance at having him, she would need to learn the art of compromise. If only she could hang on as he learned to love her, the way he'd so haltingly suggested that night on the beach.

Paige's leash loose in her hand, Isabeau walked into the nave, looking down into the church where she saw…Trystan. Unable to look away, she stared at him—so strong and formidable.

And surprisingly careful with his words.

The thought hitched—held—as she realized he wasn't the kind of man to say anything he didn't believe. Another man might have spoken of love even though he didn't feel it. But Trystan's deep wellspring of honesty prevented him from decorating his words. Cheapening them with anything but his true feelings. She admired that.

How funny that the man who'd been reputed as outspoken in this clan was simply the most honest?

Maybe a man like that was worth waiting for. Compromising for.

And loving until he loved her in all the ways she'd dreamed about.

"Presenting Mr. and Mrs. Jack Steele," Broderick Steele announced at the top of the staircase at the reception, gesturing for Jack and Jeannie to make their grand entrance after the wedding.

Glenna stood at Broderick's side, their daughter on her hip. "Welcome, Mom and Jack. We're all so happy for you both."

Trystan stood back, letting the moment roll through. He was more comfortable in the background anyway. And he was keeping his eyes on Isabeau, watching for an opening to make his case. He'd practiced what he wanted to say to her, and he hoped the wedding atmosphere would sweep her up once again, the way it had that unforgettable night in the boathouse.

He missed her today. Longed for her to be on his arm through every moment. But he'd caught glimpses of her arriving at the church, conferring with the photographers, then with the Steele and

Mikkelson women, hanging back but so very much there with Paige at her side.

Light colors and equally light tunes made the hours melt away. The beloved couple were toasted again and again. Each memory caused laughter and "awwws" from the women.

He'd done his best, making the rounds, working the reception, and now that the cake had been served, he figured he was due a moment alone on the balcony.

Not that he was cutting out completely. Just taking a breather. Unlike Royce Miller, who was conspicuously absent. That irritated Trystan. He understood that having a broken heart stunk, but this family had welcomed Royce, he worked for the company. He should have made an appearance. The gossipy whispers had to be troubling for Naomi since gossip about their breakup had spread to the press—

Holy hell, Trystan was thinking like a media person…and yes, like a man in love.

And then the hair on the back of his neck prickled with awareness. Isabeau.

He turned to find her near him, looking back at him as he stared openly at her.

She smiled, the sight so damn welcome he realized it had been days since he'd seen the real, genuine Isabeau smile and not just the pleasant working expression necessary for business. "It was a beautiful wedding. I thought they found the perfect balance in including people, but pulling off an event with no attendants other than the sons as ushers."

"If we siblings had all been groomsmen and bridesmaids, there wouldn't have been enough room on the altar for Mom and Jack."

"Well, it was beautifully done. And best of all, the women didn't have to wear ugly bridesmaid dresses." She smiled at him with emotion that reached to her eyes.

And gave him hope.

"I can't imagine anything looking ugly on you." Perhaps not the most romantic statement in the world, but he was trying.

"Thank you." Her smile wobbled a bit. "Maybe it's that pregnancy glow."

Their baby. He swallowed a lump of emotion. Of love. "If so, you wear it well."

She blushed, looking down for a moment, scratching Paige's ears in a way he'd begun to learn meant she was nervous. So he pressed ahead with small talk for now, putting his speech on hold rather than risk upsetting her. "You're right about the wedding being pretty," he continued, not wanting her to leave the balcony. "I'm not one for grand romantic gestures, but I have to confess that I was moved by how happy they both are. I didn't expect to see my mom married again, but I'm glad for her."

"You did well today. You've fulfilled your family's wishes and beyond. I'm sure they're happy and proud."

Music from the wedding reception drifted out onto the balcony, a live band performing a vintage love song.

"I owe that to you. You're an incredible teacher."

She was much more than that to him. He needed to find a way to make her understand that.

"You did the work."

"We're quite a team. At least, we were." He prayed they would be again. Any other outcome was untenable. He took her hand lightly in his, determined to make the most of this moment alone with her. "Are you still angry with me for the way I reacted when you told me about the baby?"

"I won't lie. I was hurt. But we have time to sort through things. Months, in fact."

He couldn't wait months to have her in his life. He'd missed her deeply this week. Needed to have her close to him every day going forward, for as long as she would have him.

"About that, what if we were to decide things now?"

Wariness lit her eyes, but she wasn't moving away. She squeezed his hand. "Before you launch into your latest push to get married, I have to tell you I'm tired. So can we just walk and celebrate that today was a good day, and that we're talking again?"

"I know how you like to live in the moment." He kissed her knuckles, then the inside of her wrist just over her pulse. "But the truth is, I can't go another moment without you, and I need for you to understand how much I want you in my life. Not because of the baby, but because you're…you."

She blinked up at him, her breath catching just a little, but she didn't try to interrupt him or halt him. Perhaps now was the time for his speech, after all. If only he could remember it.

He opted for the simple, amazing truth instead. "Isabeau Waters, you have turned my life upside down, but in the best of ways. Being without you even these past couple of days has made me realize I can't face spending another day apart from you. I am completely, irrevocably in love with you."

Her mouth fell open. Her fingers lifted to cover her lips for a moment. "Wow." She dropped her hand and there was something warm and wonderful in her eyes. Something that looked like possibility. "Just wow. For a man who claims not to like speeches, you have a gift."

"I have the truth of how I feel. And an inspiring muse in you." Love for her filled him all over again.

"There's no way I can match that, except to say, I feel the same. I love you and I can't deny it's scary to have my heart and happiness so connected to having you in my life. But it's more painful to think of being apart from you." She clasped his wrist and brought his palm to her stomach. "I want us to live this fairy tale and raise our child together."

He dipped his face to hers, breathing against her lips. "I am so damn glad and relieved." He stroked her stomach lightly, reverently. "Because that's exactly what I want, as well."

Then he kissed her once, twice, holding, absorbing the feel of her and the reality that they could have a future. Together. "You're glamorous and stunning and I'm scared as hell life out in the wilds of Alaska will ultimately send you running from me. I've seen what happened between Royce and Naomi. It gives me pause. I don't want these past weeks to make you think I could thrive in a city. It's not who I am."

"I don't want to change you. And I think you sell me short. I've loved seeing Alaska through your eyes. And it's not like you're a hermit living in a cave. You participate in the running of a large ranch. Your life is full."

"But what about your life? Your career? That's who you are, and I don't want to change you, either."

He'd been weighing that in his mind for weeks while they waited to see if she was pregnant, but he'd been trying to live in the moment with her, unwilling to rush. But now, they needed a workable plan for a future together.

Something rock solid that wasn't going to come unglued the way Royce and Naomi's romance was ripped at the seams. Seeing their pain made him all the more determined to get this right.

"I've been thinking about working more on a consulting basis and expanding the business with trained employees who pick up the stresses of travel so I can balance my career with motherhood." Her hand fell to rest on Paige's head, stroking the yellow Lab's velvet fur, the dog nuzzling her palm. "Paige and I were both so happy and comfortable at your ranch. I can see us thriving there."

As her words filled the space between them, he could see them coming to life. He could picture riding with Isabeau, envision her in his house and, yes, in his bed. "That sounds like a good plan, but if you find living there isn't working for you—"

"I'll tell you and we'll work on a new plan. Together." She kissed him quickly and slid her arms around his neck. "I don't want the moon and the stars. I want someone who will look at them with me. I want you to be that person."

"I do love you—" he palmed his heart "—with all that I am. Isabeau, *you* are my bucket list."

As he watched her eyes fill with happy tears of emotion, Trystan knew without question, without memorization or practice, he'd found the right words.

He'd found the right woman.

* * * * *

Get 2 Free Books,
Plus 2 Free Gifts—
just for trying the Reader Service!

HARLEQUIN *Desire*

When Lachlyn is outed as a long-lost Ballantyne heiress, wealthy security expert Reame vows to protect her. She's his best friend's sister, an innocent... Surely he can keep his hands to himself. But all it takes is one night to ignite a passion that could burn them both...

Read on for a sneak peek of
***ONE NIGHT TO FOREVER** by Joss Wood,*
*part of her **BALLANTYNE BILLIONAIRES** series!*

That damn buzz passed from him to her and ignited the flames low in her belly.

"When I get back to the office, you will officially become a client," Reame said in a husky voice. "But you're not my client...yet."

His words made no sense, but she did notice that he was looking at her like he wanted to kiss her.

Reame gripped her hips. She felt his heat and... Wow...

God and heaven.

Teeth scraped and lips soothed, tongues swirled and whirled, and heat, lazy heat, spread through her limbs and slid into her veins. Reame was kissing her, and time and space shifted.

It felt natural for her legs to wind around his waist, to lock her arms around his neck and take what she'd been fantasizing about. Kissing Reame was better than she'd imagined—she was finally experiencing all those fuzzy feels romance books described.

It felt perfect. It felt right.

Reame jerked his mouth off hers and their eyes connected, his intense, blazing with hot green fire.

She wanted him… She never wanted anybody. And never this much.

"Holy crap—"

Reame stiffened in her arms and Lachlyn looked over his shoulder to the now-open door to where her brother stood, half in and half out of the room. Lachlyn slid down Reame's hard body. She pushed her bangs off her forehead and released a deep breath, grateful that Reame shielded her from Linc.

Lachlyn touched her swollen lips and glanced down at her chest, where her hard nipples pushed against the fabric of her lacy bra and thin T-shirt. She couldn't possibly look more turned-on if she tried.

Lachlyn couldn't look at her brother, but he sounded thoroughly amused. "Want me to go away and come back in fifteen?"

Reame looked at her and, along with desire, she thought she saw regret in his eyes. He slowly shook his head. "No, we're done."

Lachlyn met his eyes and nodded her agreement.

Yes, they were done. They had to be.

Don't miss
ONE NIGHT TO FOREVER by Joss Wood,
part of her BALLANTYNE BILLIONAIRES series!

Available May 2018 wherever
Harlequin® Desire books and ebooks are sold.

www.Harlequin.com